THE ENCYCLOPAEDIA OF GOOD REASONS

THE
SEAGULL
LIBRARY OF
GERMAN
LITERATURE

THE ENCYCLOPAEDIA OF GOOD REASONS

Monica Cantieni

Translated by Donal McLaughlin

LONDON NEW YORK CALCUTTA

This publication was supported by a grant from the Goethe-Institut India

swiss arts council

prohelvetia

The original English publication of this book was supported
by a grant from Pro Helvetia, Swiss Arts Council

Seagull Books, 2021

Originally published as *Grünschnabel* by Monica Cantieni

First published in English translation by Seagull Books, 2014

ISBN 978 0 8574 2 836 3

British Library Cataloguing-in-Publication Data
A catalogue record for this book is available from the British Library.

Typeset by Seagull Books, Calcutta, India
Printed and bound by WordsWorth India, New Delhi, India

My father bought me from the council for 365 francs. That's a lot for a child without an eye in its head. I kept that bit quiet from my parents for as long as I could. If you want to be someone's daughter, destroying their hopes before you're even in through the door isn't the best idea. The Housemother hammered that into us. We can't stay with her. There are too many of us. So we have to find takers. The ones with nice eyes go quickly, ones with thick hair and good teeth. We need a good head on our shoulders too. It's the most important organ. Can replace an arm.

Not everyone's the same. For parents, the most important organ is patience.

When they came to collect me—the fresh parents were waiting at the fence, jumpier than the dog—the Housemother bent down and whispered, 'You're about to be a daughter. From there, it isn't far to a life of your own.'

They drove me and my new suitcase to their flat. They'd already had me on a trial basis, as they did, later, the plush, yellow living-room suite that took almost as long to pay off as I did. I was glad, when they were done trying me, that they decided to take me right away and only got fussy when it came to suites of furniture. Twice they sent one back. Once because of the colour. And once because of the comfort factor.

She looked out as they drove, smoked one cigarette after the other. Only occasionally did she turn round and smile, all embarrassed, ask did I like their nodding dog.

He was the exact opposite. Bombarded me with questions. What was this called, that called. Did I know this, know that. I let on to sleep.

He wanted to sound me out. They always want to know have they won the jackpot or pulled a dud.

'It can't be avoided,' the Housemother had said when, after three weeks, I returned from people who had supposedly needed a child.

They'd dropped me off a street early. Were in a hurry not to have a child any more, such was the fright I gave them. The Housemother scraped the dried tears from my cheeks.

'A child is for life.'

Did these two know that? I opened one eye, squinted at the front seats where they were sitting. Her smoking, him kneading the steering wheel. I closed my eye again.

He said, quietly, 'She has no idea about language.'

'The world's still all new to her,' she answered.

The Housemother had placed no importance on language, it gave her headaches. I was short of words. My eyes are to blame for that though. They don't see well. My new parents were concerned. They took me to the doctor to have me x-rayed, to see was my brain there.

What the doctor said, roughly, was: 'If, like me, you're not born but enter a family through a door, then certain developments can take their time.'

They refused to believe it.

HE POINTED UP TO THE SKY. The blue was full of noise.

'Look, an aeroplane.'

I screwed up my eyes, looked at his forefinger and started to sweat. I bent down, undid my shoelace and tried to tie it again. It slipped out of my fingers. I knotted it.

'Can you not see the plane?'

I did a double knot.

'OK, good,' he said. 'Come with me.'

I went back into the house behind him. We'd been standing in his pride and joy. The garden wasn't any bigger than Helene's apron—Helene's the fat cook—but thanks to my father's green fingers and cowshit, the vegetables were growing as if they were in a rush to catch the evening train to Paris.

He sat down on the sofa and tapped the cushion beside him. With an arm round me, he opened a leaflet about the airport.

'What's that, do you think?'

'Paper.'

On Saturday, he packed me into his Toyota and drove to the airport so I could see an *aeroplane*.

WE OFTEN SET OFF ON THE LOOKOUT for words. She came too but—knowing all the words already—would get bored. She smoked in the car until you could've cut through the fumes with a knife. He'd then wind the window down and she'd put on her rabbit-fur coat. She always had a plastic hood with her too. He didn't like plastic hoods. He liked the rain. Liked to feel the rain on his face and had screeds of words for it.

'I'll rattle off words as I drive and we'll collect them. *Spring rain, thundery rain, fine rain. Melted snow. Fog.* We'll take them all home. *Winds! A morning wind, an evening wind, a snow wind.* And this one—the wind you can't see in any tree, that you can only feel if you put your hand out of the window as far as your elbow. Try it and see.'

I reached out of the window and he accelerated. She shook her head.

'Careful! Think of the oncoming traffic!'

'What traffic?' he laughed.

Sometimes he'd pull up at the side of the road and write down a word for me. He often pulled up at the side of the road and wrote the word on a book of matches or an envelope, a till receipt, an empty cigarette packet. If he couldn't find anything, I'd to put my hand out and he'd write on my palm, spelling out the word. I kept the word in my hand, I kept it in my ear, then, at home, I'd cut every single one out, write each one down from my hand and sort them into matchboxes. He labelled them.

That way, they couldn't be lost. He kept them in books—*Railways of the World*, *Cold Food*, *The Seven Seas*, *Wildlife in the Congo* and *Precious Stones*—and in novels, some in two languages. The second, he rarely spoke. Only if he hit his thumb with the hammer. And if we drove into the mountains, and from there into a valley, to *Tat*. Otherwise known as Grandfather. Or *Nonno*.

'Diamonds were once wood—imagine! If you look at it like that, he said, it's our *capital* we're burning.'

Later, I put CAPITAL in a matchbox. A different one from AEROPLANE.

'Put CAPITAL in LATER, my father had said, AEROPLANE in NOW, and WIND and RAIN into ALWAYS.'

'When is ALWAYS?'

With ALWAYS, her patience snapped. She threw her cigarette out of the window and screamed at him that you don't use so much petrol learning your own language. He pulled up at the side of the road again and kneaded the steering wheel.

'So do you have a better idea?'

'Christ, buy her a pair of glasses!'

The Housemother had said it's in the nature of things that mothers are closer to practice, even if they then can't cope with it and hand it in to the Home. But at least they grappled with it for nine months first.

WE LIVED A BIT OUTSIDE THE TOWN, right on the road. The houses were as bad as my father's teeth, and a lift out of the question for the landlord. He said he wasn't Mother Teresa, and my mother complained that it was only the plaster that was holding the house together and the tenants' money problems. Living there was cheap though, and we depended on something cheap cos my father was a halfwit and not a good businessman. Neither my mother nor the rest of the relatives had noticed right away. Maybe they too had entered the family through a door and so certain developments could take their time.

MY FIRST BIRTHDAY IN THE HOUSEHOLD coincided with a bereavement on the ground floor. Death had come for the woman downstairs. I hid, to be on the safe side, not wanting to run into him. The fat cook, Helene, had warned that you're never the same afterwards, if that one crosses your path.

'You can't remember where anything is any more,' she'd said, 'not even what your own name is.'

At dawn, my mother got me out from under the bed, saying, 'Come on, there's nothing to it. She was expecting him. *Piety*—that's the most important thing now.'

'What's that?'

'Keeping calm.'

On the swing in the cage was the neighbour's bird, singing as loud as it could. My father nodded to me.

'Where were you then?'

He was on the rocking chair across from the neighbour, who was sitting, small and shrunken, on her armchair, with a book open on her lap. He wiped tears from his face.

'Page 52.'

'What?'

'She got as far as page 52. We were planning to do the Via Mala tomorrow.'

'How would you have?'

'Through binoculars, at least.'

He'd have been only too delighted to drive the woman downstairs out into the country. He'd done it once a month since her legs had given up. I always went with them cos the woman downstairs could bake a superb cake she called *Strudel*. He wanted to know every detail about it every time—about the dough, about the apples and the cherries or poppy seed in it, about the quark she called *Topfen*, while I felt sick because of the three portions I'd had and her hair lacquer that my mother used too. She piled her hair up the way my mother did, she used the same eau de cologne, they also agreed on which washing powder to use for these blouses and those skirts, it was just that the woman downstairs was partial to blouses my mother couldn't stand, even with her sunglasses on.

She bent over the armchair the woman downstairs was sitting on.

'We need some light.'

He opened the curtains, then the windows. We squinted against the sun and she said, 'My God, what a colour. And as for this pattern—incredible.'

There was nothing for me to do. As my mother was washing the woman downstairs, I fell off the chair, nearly, cos I followed the sun. It made the dust float, had a peek in the mirrors and shifted round whatever was on the floor—the shadow cast by the window, by the chairs, by a large vase, by a pile of books. It looked into the corners and even under the armchair and, once it had seen enough, vanished out of the window. I blinked and my father was looking into my face.

'Had a good sleep? Crawling away under the bed—never mind! You can have that.'

He pointed at the bird.

'Feed him. He's yours now. If the relatives call, tell them everything has been taken care of.'

The woman's relatives lived far away. They were on their way already.

They phoned, in tears, from home, they phoned from a call box, from one nearby. From a motorway services, they sobbed into the receiver, blew their noses, and someone shouted, asking, off here or the next one. The phone was ringing constantly and I'd to repeat myself. They called to hear how the woman downstairs was and I told them all she was dead and there was nothing but piety, my mother's washing her and my father's cooking, as sure as eggs is eggs and the food's heavenly.

'We're driving with a vengeance,' they said.

They don't have much time. The woman downstairs wants to become ashes. She has to be put in the ground in a tin.

CURTAINS WERE PULLED BACK, people settled on cushions in the window, scratched their heads, greeted those who had remained outside and were shaking their heads at cars turning into the street with their exhausts roaring and pulling up on the kerb. As they arrived—horns blowing, engines roaring, doors slamming. Then—cursing, crying, paper rustling in the hall. My mother felt like howling. But what was she to do? They were coming from far away, had brought lilies, wine, bunches of creaky gladioli they turned in their hands until the flowers started falling off and my mother said, 'Come on in.'

Beside my bed my birthday present was piled high—the fattest encyclopaedia, in fifteen volumes. On A-BAU, teeth were fizzing in a glass. I wasn't sleeping alone. Two of the woman-down-below's sisters were in my bed. One on my left and one on my right. They were so broad, the bed creaked each time they drew breath. Uncles and sons were lying in the hall, in the living room were more relatives—a human carpet in their socks and coats, their hats down over their faces. The gladioli had been put in buckets, and in the hall, wreaths were piled up like car tyres. The lily scent was hanging in the rooms, it stuck to your palate, couldn't be shifted, was sweet and heavy like the two old cronies who were snoring. The glass with the teeth fizzed and the bed grunted. Those two had forgotten me, they held each other's hands, wet—time and again—with tears.

My mother took a hellish misery pill. She opened the door to see the Peroxide Blonde from next door with her arm round three yapping dogs and slammed it in her face again. Later, she went over with cake and two guests and, not knowing what else to do with them, forced the cake and guests on the Peroxide Blonde. Specially selected, the guests were. One had bleached hair too. Common interests can help break the ice.

There was a lot of running round in the hall. Everyone dressed in black. Everyone in high spirits. The neighbours greeted my mother: 'What a beautiful funeral.' My mother greeted them back: 'Far too expensive.'

A few neighbours had forgotten they didn't get on with me. They touched my hair. The Peroxide Blonde led the way, letting me pet her dogs.

'When Death's involved,' my mother said, 'people tend not to take things so seriously. Some let go so much, they hit rock bottom.'

'It will all sort itself out,' my father said, 'at the meal.'

The kitchen was his when it came to a big crowd. And the weekend his, anyway. The woman downstairs had had the good fortune to die on the Thursday and the relatives, luckily, were a large group—a double jackpot. My father was already very excited. In his mind, was peeling mountains of potatoes, cutting vegetables and cutting up a cow and some chickens and pigs that had found dying easier than the woman downstairs. Far easier.

'It's a surprise for them,' he said, 'to wake up on Pig Cloud, in Cow Heaven or among the Chicken Stars. From up there, they look proudly down on these pans and are amazed: You don't say! That one there, that's me, and there's my brother-in-law. Astonishing—something became of the stupid pig, after all. And here—look what you can do with a silly cow. Incredible.'

My father wanted the kitchen to himself. But my mother was wiping breadcrumbs from the sideboard, off the table, she mopped under the table, she found socks. She gave the TV a wipe, found a hat, three hats, a fourth on the birdcage. She wiped as much as she could since everyone was out, getting some air, going for a walk. My father was walking up and down, writing lists, and finally went to the shops.

He wasn't to exaggerate, she called after him, knowing he couldn't slip off his hospitality even to go to bed. No, just bring them all back, for God's sake, anyone you find in the street, in doorways or under a stone.

She found herself crying a little as his knows-no-limits hospitality was too much for her and she could already see herself eating bills again, just to get rid of them.

My mother walked through the lily scent, dividing it with eau de cologne. She'd got dressed up meanwhile. She set the table. For two days now, she'd been setting the table almost constantly, and on the third, she needed all the plates—all those she had, and all those she could get. Plates were compulsory. No one came without one, and my father stood in the kitchen watching Eli flattening the schnitzels.

My father liked to watch Eli. Eli was a brickie who normally did piecework. He'd hands that were as large as frying pans and his sense of proportion was highly regarded by others in his field. But people talked about Eli nevertheless. Even in the government. It wasn't clear whether the government allowed him Switzerland or not. Even though there was nothing he couldn't do. His blocks of flats were as good as his hutch for Snow White. He could make things like that in his sleep, and by day often visited us to be of great help. My father didn't care that people were talking and the fact the government even wrote letters about Eli really didn't impress him.

'Idiots. Without exception. Stupid fools. The government can shove it!'

He lifted me onto the sideboard. Coating was crumbling from his hands.

'Sure, look at Eli. Eliseo Álvaro Manuel Raúl Caballero Pardo. He's an able man, am I right?'

I was waiting. My father was going to explain Cow Heaven properly to me.

'It's like this, you see. In Cow Heaven, the animals have to budge up. Some people go up there too when they die, without anyone noticing. It's the same with the pigs and the chickens. Blunders like that can happen.'

Is it any wonder? All those heavens. How can anyone know their way round? And then there's Pepperland. It's a paradise while you're still alive, where my father sometimes wanted to send my mother to take a cure. It never worked out though. There was never ever enough money in our house.

The door was open. It was never closing now. My mother made her way through the guests, counting them. In the hall, the toilet, the different rooms. She found two in the marital bed that weren't in the mood for a schnitzel but were gobbling each other up and spilling schnapps—the meal hadn't even been served yet. She counted in the living room and in the kitchen, those who were pounding the meat, thrashing it such that the tendons swelled. She called to them, 'It's a disgrace—in our bed.'

Eli started to roll up his sleeves. My father held him back.

'Leave it. Let them eat first.'

My mother shook her head. She was now going round with bottles. She took another two hellish misery pills, then started counting all over again. She ordered me and the Peroxide Blonde round the flat with bowls and glasses and told the gladioli:

'They're not even all here yet.'

Dejan and Mirela were missing. The best-looking couple, far and wide. They were still stuck in the restaurant where they worked. They'd be coming later, with roast pork and Dejan's guitar that livened things up in his spare time. Henry and Silvester should've arrived long since too. They'd come here from Africa cos Switzerland needed them to produce huge blade wheels that foreign countries used to make electricity, my father said. Henry and Silvester had gone from Africa to America, to attend the school for blade wheels and electricity. In their rooms, they'd square hats with cords that were gathering dust on cushions, and on the walls were framed papers. In America, they'd earned a reputation that reached as far as Europe, and they'd come to Switzerland on a red carpet. Henry and Silvester were indispensable for Swiss industry. Blade wheels were the top seller. Eli also said the pair had been hand-picked. Only my mother wasn't impressed by that. On the contrary—every time my father tried to talk about Henry and Silvester, the dishes would rattle in the kitchen cupboard as noisily as when he mentioned Uncle Gion who wasn't right in the head, or a neighbour, a woman who had a love supermarket in Zurich.

My father dished up the schnitzels and my mother checked everything was in order. Given that the marital bed had been desecrated, you could now expect everything and anything, she said. And it was true—live chickens, for example, hanging from the shower head, tied together in a bouquet that beat its wings when she released it.

'Eli!'

She carried them into the kitchen. One fell to the floor, picked itself up, fluttered over their heads. The Peroxide Blonde had to restrain her dogs. The chicken was agitated, was dispensing feathers and shit. One of the woman-down-below's cousins caught it and reached under its feathers. She pressed it down into the flowers on her dress till it calmed down and let her put it in her bag. There, it peeked out between the teeth of the zip and was as quiet as a mouse.

EVENTUALLY, MIRELA AND DEJAN ARRIVED TOO. Mirela was beaming for two, she always did. Her skin was as white as the milk that, in the cellar of the restaurant, she stirred until it turned to cheese and squeezed through cloths. The pair had a crate of Slibowitz with them, Violin-Goran, Dejan's guitar, and the pork in the form of a whole pig that my mother ran away from. Dejan held the greasy parcel out to me.

'What's wrong with her? It's fresh. And still warm. How come she doesn't like suckling pig?'

'She can't eat children.'

He shrugged his shoulders, shoved his way past, opened a jar of paprika purée Mirela had handed him, piled some round loaves on the table, tucked a plate under his arm, put cutlery in his jacket pocket, then went over to the phone and dialled the number with his fork. It was while eating that Dejan missed the language from home most. He was phoning friends. Pulling the cord behind him, he walked round the rooms, speaking, until the connection was suddenly lost. Dejan was shaking the receiver and tapping the mouthpiece, trying to get the last of the words to drop out, when someone tore open the door and threw the cord at his feet. He held the guitar out to Dejan.

'Get a move on. Come in and play, will you?'

Dejan kept the promise others had made. What music. Even my mother and the Peroxide Blonde danced until they were dizzy and others would've had to hold them up, had the flat not been as full as the Number 4 bus. Every now and then, someone toppled out of the door, remained sitting in the stairwell and fell asleep. Not one noticed me popping wrinkly black olives into their ears. Dejan swore by this when he wanted peace and quiet.

Inside, Dejan had an arm round his guitar, and Eli, an arm round Dejan. They had big emotions and were singing when I carried the cake in. It was just like the old cronies had said—everyone got out of the way, they made space. Heaven knows where they found it. They held their stomachs in as if the bride was arriving.

Just one pushed his hat back off his head.

'What am I supposed to want with that?'

He turned his back to the cake, put his hand on a schnitzel to take its temperature. He clicked his tongue, said 'Cold', then 'Doesn't matter', and ate it out of his hand.

'What's your name?'

'Johann.'

'Where are you from?'

'Hernals.'

'Where's Hernals?'

'Hernals, the 17th district.'

'17th district, where?'

'Vienna. Austria.'

Johann dabbed his lips with a paper hankie. My father and Eli joined him.

'The best, eh, those were the very best schnitzel I've had in my life.—But tell me, what's the *tschusch* doing here?'

'What's a *tschusch*?'

'One of them.'

Johann pointed at Dejan.

'A Slav.—Have you niggers too?'

My father didn't say a word. He didn't even explain what a *tschusch* is.

'IT'S YOUR BEDTIME.'

'I don't want to go.'

'They're all drinking. It happens as fast as a sunset in the tropics—you hardly blink and the sun's away and the night has come and it brings people down.'

'Where are Henry and Silvester?'

‘You know fine.’

‘I’m going to call him Bird.’

‘Who?’

‘The bird.’

‘That’s not a proper name.’

‘Will you think of one?’

‘Yes.’

‘Will you write it down for me?’

‘Tomorrow, once the guests have gone.’

His hands forgot the promise. They were otherwise engaged. They always were. That day, for example, they’d ruffled the fur of the Peroxide Blonde’s dogs, shampooed the Toyota, beaten schnitzels, rested on my mother’s hips in the kitchen and, in the stairwell, on Henry and Silvester’s shoulders, to encourage them a bit to go cos it wasn’t just Johann—my mother was allergic to Africa too.

'SUCH A SWEET LITTLE THING.'

Aunt Joujou had come specially, all the way from the village below the Churfirsten, to say that.

She repeated herself.

'A sweet thing. And so pretty. Where did you get the like?'

On the table were two incredibly thin, long loaves. Aunt Joujou swore by them. *Baguettes*, they were called. There was a runny cheese, too, that she called *ripe* though it hadn't come from the garden. Mother's side of the family, my father said, Mother's side comes from France. Mother's side is completely mad, he said. And unbearable.

Aunt Joujou started to stir her coffee. She'd been given the nicest cup. The one with a wide-eyed deer peeking out of a forest while a hunter points a rifle at it. My father called it a classical hunting scene. On the saucer, the deer was already dead. And lying on fir branches, waiting for the chef.

High and clear, the tinkle of the spoon. Quiet too. Like Aunt Joujou's voice that wanted to know whether my background had been investigated cos you could catch something from children with a background. As the wife of a pharmacist, she'd have wanted to know, and one thing was sure—I might be a little dark but there was a good chance I'd grow out of it. She sighed and stroked my hair. Nibbling a biscuit, she went on to say this and that while my father kneaded the bridge of his nose and tested the spring on a tablecloth clip. My mother was drumming her fingers and threw a few squashed olives onto the table.

'From the hall, they are. There were more there. A lot, to be exact. I swept them out of all the corners today, all these black wrinkly things. They'd made their way into the cracks, and I'd to scrape them out. And it wasn't as if I'd nothing else to do, what with the funeral.'

Aunt Joujou was stirring her coffee and making it splash into the saucer. She didn't like to be interrupted. Sweeping what remained of the olives into a pile, my mother said, 'That said, it was a beautiful funeral. Really beautiful, I must say. With a lot of flowers. Lots of flowers. And lots of people, as is only right. Not all top-notch, you have to admit, but you can't choose your relatives, not even if you're as posh as the woman downstairs was. She liked to read, she died with a book in her hand, could afford to as well—sit around, reading books. Not that I'd have begrudged her it. She was exceedingly pleasant. Incredible, how many books we found in the flat. Not to mention the cellar. And the attic. Whole wall units full. Boxes, crates, suitcases—filled with books. Nothing but books. And these blouses. In colours you wouldn't have thought possible.'

Aunt Joujou didn't look up from the cup she was stirring. Quite the opposite—she seemed to want to inspect it more closely, as if she'd just noticed the hunting scene.

'Very nicely made. Is it a one-off?'

When my mother started playing with the olive mush again, she looked for a long time at the deer waiting for the chef before slurping up the contents of the saucer.

'Listen: remaining childless is no rarity. There's many an unfortunate case like you. You don't need to let it upset you.'

The Housemother had said that too. Unfortunate cases like my mother, and all their organs, are first offered medical care. If that's a dead loss, they turn to the Church to see if there's a God. If the God can't help either, it's then our turn.

'The same goes for unfortunate cases like the little one. Don't think anything of it.'

When the cup hit the wall next to Aunt Joujou, my father rubbed his brow and started checking the second tablecloth clip. Moving round the kitchen, my mother collected every last thing Aunt Joujou had brought with her—the baguettes, her coat, the travel bag, the cheese, a scarf, hat, shoes, magazines, flowers—and threw it all out of the window. Down in the street, bicycle bells rang and horns tooted, a brake squealed and someone screamed: 'Foreign scum!' My father repeatedly depressed the spring-loaded clip.

IN THE TOILET, IT'S QUIET. You can think your thoughts without being disturbed. I waited outside, to help my mother a bit. She'd finally stopped crying.

'Aunt Joujou's gone.'

'Good.'

'They're all gone.'

'Good.'

'Should I go and get the Peroxide Blonde?'

'Definitely not.'

'And Eli?'

'Not him either.'

'Should I phone Tat?'

'You're to phone no one.'

I looked across into the living room, at my father.

'Do you want to speak to him?'

'No. Where is he anyway?'

'Lying on the sofa.'

'How is he?'

'He has a headache, he says. And we need new tablecloth clips. Three of them.'

My mother started crying again.

'Are tablecloth clips so expensive?'

'Give me five minutes' peace, would you. Would you all just give me peace.'

I stayed put for a while. Sometimes my mother changed her mind, wanted me to fetch her hellish misery pills, a glass of water and her favourite magazine.

'On you go. Get away.'

My father turned round on the sofa and closed his eyes so as not to have to see it. Now the sofa belonged to him, he no longer liked it. A mustardy-yellow nightmare was what he called it, which is what I was the next day too, as I puked up the little bit of meat and puked up the spot of mashed potato, the half a banana, the rice, the cup of soup, the spoonful of gruel. My mother shook her head, felt my forehead, took the small bowl, the plate, the glasses out. I was being steamed in socks soaked in warm water and vinegar. The Peroxide Blonde came to visit, so did Eli and Mirela and, later, Dejan.

They stand round the bed.

'Would you look at that.'

'It's clearly the liver.'

'Clearly.'

'As yellow as a golden Jerusalem.'

'As yellow as a sunflower.'

'As yellow as a yellow pepper.'

'A brimstone butterfly.'

'Butter.'

They shake their heads, walk up and down the room.

'Some heat in here.'

'An oppressive heat.'

'A sweltering heat.'

'An excessive heat.'

They feel my brow. The doctor does too.

'Boiling hot.'

'Burning hot.'

'And damp.'

'Wet.'

'Wringing wet.'

'Soaking wet.'

'Drenched.'

'Incredible.'

They shuffle their feet, and Eli goes with them to the door. The doctor too, who comes and goes and whispers, closes the door gently. The phone that rings, the ring that echoes, my head that gets warm and warmer and hot. My father said Tat had phoned, wanting to know how I was. My mother shook her head. Eli's hand on my shoulder, holding the receiver for me and whispering, 'Your grandfather.'

'Tat?'

'Yes.'

Tat who asks how it's going, who tells me the plums are incredibly big this year, huge and juicy, the apples a dream. The receiver falls from my hand.

My head, and the roar in it.

My head that crackles and creaks, that is beating in time. Tat, who falls out of the tree, who throws apples at plums, at the clock on his roof, at his legs that dance in the kitchen without him.

Light that comes and goes.

Eli's gaze that settles on me, and his hand that takes mine. A bobbing light in the window, light in Eli's eyes, a spark that goes out, Eli asleep.

Hands that change. That don't let go. Not for three days, they say. Three days.

On the fourth, I'm sitting at the kitchen table, supping soup. Maybe she wants to stay. My mother strokes my hair.

'Be better soon.'

They watched me eating, took turns at that too, my mother cut flowers, put them in a vase, my father was reading, and later, my mother took the coat. She came back with a box that she unpacked on my bed. My father put his book down.

'What's that?'

'A sun lamp.'

'What do we need that for?'

'My complexion.'

'Your complexion?'

My mother looked first at him, then at me.

'I didn't do anything.'

My father rubbed the wings of his nose.

'I know. It was Mother Nature.'

It had also been Mother Nature who had given this flu to almost everyone. Only my parents, Eli and the Peroxide Blonde didn't fall ill, it was a miracle. They all had their hands full with things to do. My father was making chicken soup non-stop, my mother delivered it and came home with baskets full of bed linen that she washed at night. The Peroxide Blonde didn't even have time to have her hair done. Her parting was ginger as, without a word, she ironed the washing in our kitchen and gave her three big ones a clout if they goggled at the TV instead of doing their homework.

After the flu, everyone was sick out of sheer tiredness. My mother needed even more peace and quiet and to be shown consideration. She had to groom herself. After a full hour in front of the sun lamp, she lay down on the deckchair with a paste made of cucumber, honey and quark on her face. I looked quietly up at the sky, drew on tiptoe and took all the words out to Eli, who was sitting at the hutch, feeding Snow White stale bread. My collection in matchboxes was already pretty big. Words for LATER, from BEFORE, for NOW.

ADOPTION was the word for what I had. Eli had explained it to me. It was my newest word.

'But it won't fit in the NOW box.'

'Then take out CARE. You don't need that any more.'

'I do.'

'Then put it into the future box. There's still a lot of space in that one.'

My mother had written ADOPTION. My father, CAPITAL. Eli wrote AT HOME.

'And where does HAPPINESS go?'

'Life's not obliged to provide that.'

'And ADOPTION?'

'Not that either.'

'Write HAPPINESS for me.'

HAPPINESS. It belongs in the matchbox IMPROBABILITY oblique HOPE.

'And LIFE?'

'Belongs in every box.'

Eli wrote down LA VIDA.

'Is it the same in Spanish?'

'It's not the same in any tongue.'

Not all the flats in our building had central heating. So, in winter, most people used electric heaters. There were difficulties with the electricity, everybody wanted some, but the house hadn't been planned with so many tenants in mind.

By night, the men wired us up to the house next door, and fuses went left, right and centre. Not every radiator was legally present, not to mention the TVs and radios.

There was an uproar any time the ones next door discovered, again, that our radios, TVs and even heating had been running on their electricity. Once they did, it would be dark, cold and quiet in nearly every flat again after the police had ripped the wires out. Also, there were problems—not only too many radiators had been standing around the flats illegally, too many foreigners had too. Unlucky, my father called them, and lucky beggars those that Eli had waved out of the back door and driven to a vacation on a far-away building site so they'd not be a burden on the electricity here until such times as things had calmed down again.

The landlord sympathized with the foreigners—was sympathetic to more coming because they belong together, to more coming because they are born, to them all wanting somewhere to go. He'd nothing against them wanting to increase in size.

'A pleasure shared is twice as great,' he said.

The foreigners understood him.

They called Eli, and he erected a wall, made two flats out of one. Following which the landlord's pleasure was twice as great and the foreigners' was shared.

Once a week, he came to collect the rent. With his hands in his bulging pockets, he repeated in the stairwell that the foreigners' prospects lay in their modesty. That earned him a lot of names. My father called him an asshole, and if he didn't get a punch in the teeth, it was only because Eli was next to him. Even my mother called him a swine at the table and Eli said, 'Eso cabrón! Es un hombrecito sin cojones.'

When it came from the heart like that, Eli's Spanish interested my mother. Something that sounded lovely—like the name of a fancy pie that the neighbourhood gave you a doctorate for—was something she'd have been glad to include in her collection.

'What's that?'

Eli explained to my mother that the landlord didn't have any, and she asked, 'What then?'

Eli explained you could cut off the landlord's balls and he wouldn't notice because he hasn't got any, or—to put it another way—because he hasn't any guts, and my mother said she couldn't have balls at the dinner table as they're bad for a girl of my age. I already knew all about balls though. Did she think I'd been living on the moon? Balls are widely used and, unless they fall foul of the law, aren't particularly interesting, the House-mother had said.

Eli wanted to add something but my mother was giving him a look. And if my mother gave him a look, my father's soufflé would collapse, fuses would go, something would cave in or break down, and my father said flowers in vases would then wither faster and if things were really bad, their heads would fall off right away.

ON SUNDAYS, ELI HAD TO FEED SNOW WHITE and Bird and close the windows if it rained. On Sundays, we drove to Tat's.

Tat Jon, who plays chess, against himself, if necessary. Tat, who, even in his old age, still cooks, who stirs soft cheese into his polenta, who cleans his motorbike though he can no longer drive it, who doesn't blame his motorbike though it cost him one of his legs.

Tat, who smokes Toscanis and is in the doldrums, who farts fruit and can't digest things properly, though that's not his motorbike's fault.

Tat, who is all yellow and grey. His hair, his moustache, his fingers, his nails. His rooms—empty riverbeds, dried-up lakes, yellow like in Africa where, every year, for more than six months, the rivers and lakes go on holiday.

Tat Jon, whose second leg went up in smoke.

Tat, who wants to get up during the night to make polenta, to shit polenta, to make coffee, to piss coffee or blood.

Tat, who has more clocks in the house than knives and forks and spoons, all showing different times, to try and fool Death. A house full of ticking and purring and buzzing noises, and you can hear the cuckoo calling. Just like in the forest, while a fire is smoking, or the polenta is cooking, or the windows are open, it seems, just for the wasps.

Tat, who only washes the front of the plates.

Tat, who has to leave the house when my mother comes to tidy up, make the beds, beat the carpets and take the shelves apart, the fridge, wipe the black-and-white tiles on the floor, wash the knives and forks and spoons, and the backs of the plates.

Tat, who doesn't want to leave when she comes. Till my mother gives him a look. Tat, who then takes a dander round the house, giving all the clocks that have stopped a nudge.

Tat, who has more wrinkles than a stalk of celery and ears with tufts of hair that make it hard to hear. Tat, whose wrinkles on his neck tremble like a turkey's.

Tat, who cries when he falls, even his old dog can walk better than him. His dog, a one-and-only, has been fetching help since my Tatta's been gone—Sepp. Sepp, who is as undemanding as grass.

Tat, who cooks a lot and washes little, who slurps his coffee from the saucer, who sits outside, who sucks strawberries, raspberries and blackberries, who splits apricots, and peaches, who cuts apples and pears, leaves the nuts to the crows, doesn't notice when winter comes and it's cold in the garden—my parents shake their heads.

Tat, who needs more than fifteen minutes to go down to the cellar and back again. Tat will die. No one is as close to Death as he is.

Tat, who has five legs. One that fits, one that chafes, and one in prospect—the one he fights with the insurance about—one he can feel even though it's gone and one he remembers fondly because it calms him down.

Tat. Or Nonno. Or Grandfather. Depending on who is visiting. A godforsaken place the devil couldn't care less about, folks say. The bends we take to get there are incredible. I get sick every time.

'LOOK AT THAT.'

Tat wasn't happy with his legs. He wanted a third one, had ordered one from the insurance but they didn't want to send him any more.

Where he should've had a left leg, there was a second right and that caused problems at the shoe shop. Tat caused problems at the shoe shop but not just there—also for the insurance company that had got him into this in the first place. He wrote to them once a week, more often if his stump got sore. He wrote by hand. My father had removed the keys on the typewriter you need for *defamation of an official*. Defamation had cost Tat a lot of money. The insurance company was now holding out the prospect of something else to him: *certification*.

Every Sunday, my father had to read all the replies from the insurance company to him, even if nothing new had arrived. Tat forgot things quickly. He wanted his head to be up-to-speed again and so was looking for his glasses. Without them, he couldn't listen. While my father leafed through the letters and read them out, Tat would grind his jaws, suck his loose dentures and snarl.

'Merda de giat! Catshit!'

'Don't curse like that.'

'The hell I will. My guts are rattling. Is anything of yours hurting?'

'Yes, a tooth.'

'You still have it though. Even things I'm missing are hurting me.'

'Why do you need even more legs, Tat?'

'You can see, sure, Whippersnapper—I keep falling.'

'And how come the insurance won't buy you a new one?'

'I'm not another wonder of the world, it says. No one needs more than two legs.'

'Can you not buy yourself one?'

Tat shakes his head.

'Too dear.'

'But why have you two right legs? No one else does.'

'That's just what I'm saying. Check out this little Whippersnapper. She has more grey matter than a whole insurance company.'

'Why have you two right legs?'

'I had a motorbike accident. Years ago now. I lost a leg as a result. After the accident, I was given one leg, a right one. It didn't fit properly. I was given another one, was pretty happy with it, put the first away in a cupboard, then I lost my other leg.'

'I know. Clogged veins caused by too many Toscanis.'

Tat shifted to and fro on his seat, as if something had stung him.

'Would you look at Whippersnapper! Whatever—the insurance company has two legs recorded in its files. No one can ask for more than that, they say. Two legs are two legs. When are you all leaving? We've not been in the garden yet.'

The garden had too much fruit. The plums were the size of peaches. The apples, a deep red. The trees were bending over, there was so much fruit. We loaded it into the car by the basketful. The Peroxide Blonde raved about Tat's fruit. In our street, it was world famous. Tat was delighted. Ever since he'd started delivering free fruit to the town, the townsfolk no longer looked down on him so much.

'Why?'

'Because. But there are also better reasons.'

Tat and I started the Encyclopaedia of Good Reasons. By the end of the afternoon, it had more pages than I was able to count yet and Tat could still remember. Tat also called good reasons *arguments*. *Arguments* could change colour. Good *arguments*, as fast as the wind, were unbeatable and just like the special knives of the doctors who had tried to save Uncle Niculin's heart. Sometimes, not even good reasons or the best *arguments* can help, Tat said. But some things were certain—there are good reasons for plum trees, for peach trees, for strawberry cake, for fast motorbikes, Toscanis, for beautiful women, very beautiful women and especially beautiful women (Tat), for moments that seem like eternity, when your heart stops with happiness, for long kisses (I'd no idea what Tat was talking about, actually he didn't any more either, he said). All the more because of those things, there were good reasons for memory, for now, even if you can't always see it. There are good reasons for Dejan's music, for Mirela's laugh, for warm bread, Eli's walls, artificial parents, artificial legs, for schnitzel, for Snow White, good weather and fly swatters.

There were good reasons for the Housemother, for her dog, for metal grilles on windows and extra-warm blankets, for pudding on Sunday and stewed apple, for Helene's cake, for apples that are stolen and those given to you, for a black eye or two, for getting your ears boxed, there were good reasons for big people to dish out punishments, for little ones to tell tales, there were good reasons for those who ran away and for those who stayed out.

'There are even good reasons for flies,' Tat says. 'If they didn't eat so much shit, there'd be even more of it in the world.'

WITH HIS TEETH BACK IN THE GLASS ALREADY, he said good-bye and, talking to himself, he stood in the doorway, raised his hand, and my father sighed, this time can always be the last. My mother sighed too. Now Tat would again forget the polenta he'd made or make a new one every day, always a whole pan so he could use it the following day too, he'd forget which day it was, not eat anything after all and, at some point, puzzled, look for the polenta beneath the mould and then phone while making a new batch. He'd the time to as he stirred.

POLENTA, I put in the ALWAYS box. It should always be fresh, always be ready and waiting for Tat.

NEW TENANTS MOVED INTO THE BUILDING. They made a lot of noise. Together with the noise us children made, that really got on my mother's nerves. Her nerves may have been made of steel but she was also at the end of them. Here, everyone was at the end of their nerves—the Peroxide Blonde with her sons, especially. We'd been gunning for her dogs, you see. Her lads had taken one to bleach it. She made a huge fuss cos her hair was bleached too, and her Werner, Long-Distance Werner, always abroad with his lorry, alone on a country road, and her inconsolable somehow.

She set her bulk in motion, puffed her way up the stairs, shouting that she'd be putting her lads in a home and we wouldn't be far behind them, and that she cursed herself for not abandoning us all at motorway services years ago, or telling her husband to take us off abroad somewhere too. Then she slammed the door. Bits of plaster fluttered down—which surprised no one. The women in the building banged doors an incredible lot, the landlord let them, and once a year, you'd see the men in the hall with their putty, patching it up.

Occasionally, one of the new tenants would come towards you in the stairwell. His skin was as dark as mine.

'There's something not right with him,' my mother said.

'He's Italian,' said my father.

'His name is Toni,' I said.

'How do you know?'

'I was in the garden.'

'Oh, he was in the garden?'

'He says he needs fresh veg. He plants it. He says working with the soil is as honest as having children. It's just—you don't always arrive at soil and children in honest fashion.'

You could've cut the air with a knife. My father crammed me full of words and then they went out of my head again at the most unfavourable moments.

The subject of having children, quite simply, wasn't good for my mother's appetite. I should've known. It lay in her stomach, was as heavy as a killer fondue. She felt full immediately. She pushed her plate away and said slowly that my father couldn't have children. My father said my mother couldn't either. And it wasn't known how I came about. My mother said I'd been lying ready in the hospital, had been travelling somehow and could've been fetched at any moment, but because that hadn't happened over an extended period, I'd ended up elsewhere, which was where they got me. The End. My father sighed, muttered he'd a toothache, said work was calling, and she said, yes, yes, on you go, so quietly he didn't hear her. She took a hellish misery pill but it didn't help. She lay down, sent me into the kitchen for another pill but it wasn't any use either, she just felt worse. She told me that at my age she'd also travelled, the war being on at the time. France had been no longer habitable cos of the Germans. There were pictures in her head that wouldn't go away. Incredible, she said, after all these years. The pictures remained—some of French railway stations, some of trains. Pictures of uncles that weren't there when you needed them. Of houses that weren't there when you needed them. Houses that had blown up in her uncles' faces, her aunts' faces, her uncles' faces, even a brother's, when he was still a child. Everything in bits, thousands of bits, she said. Everything. Those who survived were scattered all over the world now. Those who had got away, the few lucky ones. And relatives. For example, here. Blood is thicker than water. That is to say, war leaves nothing standing, not one stone on top of another, not a single picture as it was. Especially not that. Not during the day even. And particularly, not at night.

'Be glad you don't know anything about the war that all these ones know nothing about. They haven't a clue.'

She looked at me.

'Let's go.'

'Where?'

'To beneath the biggest tree with the best view.'

She'd yet to take me there. Until now, she'd only ever gone alone and returned in a good mood.

'I'll make sandwiches for us.'

'And then we'll go to the zoo?'

'If you like.'

'And I can have an ice-cream?'

'And you can have an ice-cream.'

'And we'll also go to Almost-No-Feathers?'

'If you want, also to Almost-No-Feathers.'

'I'll take an orange for him.'

Beneath the biggest tree with the best view, there was nothing to see but graves. My mother was very satisfied. Once the last church bell had stopped, she took out the sandwiches and laboriously unwrapped two.

'From up here you really do have the best view. My funeral—'

Bread was crumbling on her rabbit-fur coat, she was speaking with her mouth full.

'Want one?'

I shook my head.

'My funeral will be an event, I guarantee you that. Flowers as far as the eye can see and more wreaths than the woman downstairs got. Even Peter Alexander will send one and the biggest will be from Gustav Knuth. Everyone pushes towards the coffin. It's lowered carefully, very carefully, as if they were planting a rare flower, yes, exactly like that.'

Behind us, in the biggest tree, birds were quarrelling. She kept her eyes closed, sat there, bolt-upright, as if in front of her sun lamp, and spread her arms out. The sandwich wrapper blew away.

'And then the brass band plays the Radetzky March. And everyone has come. Everyone. I've chosen the people carefully, believe me. Don't go thinking I'll invite just anyone, there's a list, a small, special selection, and still, the cemetery's bursting at the seams. They're standing on top of one another, as far back as the gate, some are even standing on other graves. Five minutes of that and the concierge's grave already looks like it's been ploughed. Even the lousy wooden cross, with the varnish flaking off, isn't bearing up. Sure no one can see where they're stepping, their eyes are all so puffed-up from crying already. They trample the cross into the mud. It's as if no cross had ever stood there, as if it had never been there, as if he'd never been there. Incredible. The guy from the newspaper's standing there, shaking his head, taking a photo. This has never happened here before. If only you could see all the people in the picture. The lens isn't good enough. But he doesn't have another one with him. He's not here from Hollywood, after all. Unlike Clark Gable, who has come all this way, arriving at the last minute. Johannes Heesters and Cary Grant are already sobbing at the coffin. Clark's completely out of breath. He conceals it well though. Is an actor, after all. If you like, you can ask for an autograph.'

She looked down briefly at me as she unwrapped her third sandwich, then had half the town ploughed over for the hotels for the guests from all over the world. By the time her sandwich was finished, there was another funeral, at the foot of the Churfirsten, with a band and a table, metres long, with a white tablecloth and a view of the Walensee. A Mr Tony Curtis was bowled over. She pulled her rabbit-fur round her tighter and put on her sunglasses, as you do at funerals.

'The priest can hardly get a word out. What's he supposed to say anyway? Slowly, it dawns on him, something like an enlightenment, my goodness, such a crowd, they've all come because they know who is lying there before them, he—'

'Do the dead lie here for ever?'

'What? No. They throw them away. After twenty-five years.'

'Why?'

'For reasons of space.'

'Will I throw you away too when you've been dead for twenty-five years?'

My mother opened her eyes, wiped the crumbs from her rabbit-fur coat. She looked at me.

'The groundsman does it.'

'And then what?'

'The memory remains.'

'Can that be thrown away too?'

'Not really.'

'Can the groundsman do it?'

'He can't either.'

The rows of stones and crosses were long, between them paths, orange watering cans, fountains, bending trees. The biggest tree was rustling, and beneath it, the flowers and bouquets all pointed in the same direction.

'When are we going to the zoo?'

'Soon.'

She lit a cigarette, smoked it, lit a second, put the collar of her coat up. Occasionally, she shook her head, looking at me from the side as if I were something special.

The zoo had no sharks, just carp you could only see in winter cos, in summer, the algae and soaked bread made the water murky. There was a fat snake that didn't move, apart from on Sundays when, at half past two, guinea pigs would vanish inside it, and it would then look like a car tyre. Then there were two monkeys with beards and a stuffed lion that, at 3.15 p.m., roared over the tannoy and so all round the zoo. There were also budgies, a bit where guinea pigs were bred, two goats, and rabbits that holed up when the lion roared at 3.15.

Almost-No-Feathers was also known as an African grey parrot and had a cage to himself at the far end of the zoo. The zookeeper called that an *aviary*, and explained that Almost-No-Feathers would've been able to fly in it if he didn't look like a plucked chicken you'd just removed from the fridge. He'd been plucking his feathers out ever since the other parrot died. *Secretly*, the zookeeper said, never when someone's around.

My mother was afraid of him, almost as much as of swans, cos he'd push up really close to the bars and his unblinking yellow eyes would just gawp at everyone. He was famous for waiting at the bars, as stock still as the stuffed lion, then pecking at any fingers that reached in before he'd bristled his head feathers. Then, the zookeeper had said, *then* you may. But not before. And bring some fruit.

If I called his name, he'd go back and forth on his branch, all excited, then hop up to the bars, stick a foot and his beak out and coo like a pigeon. For the whipped cream on my strawberry ice-cream, the zookeeper had whispered to me, the thing would learn how to shoot even.

THE FIRST TIME THE ONES FROM WELFARE CAME, they knelt in front of me and suggested I use their first names. Ever since ADOPTION had been put in my LATER matchbox, they'd been dropping by to see how things were progressing.

Ruth smelt of apples and was less than a quarter of the size of Walter who was so out of breath you'd've thought he'd galloped his way to us. He wiped his face with a hankie, leant, exhausted, on the sideboard, sipped at his coffee and immediately drank a litre of water. Welfare seemed to be in the middle of a desert. He let Ruth ask the questions and he wrote the report. Ruth wanted to know was I well, and I picked fresh dandelion in the garden, took her to the hutch, showed her Snow White, talked about the zoo, and Ruth stroked Snow White's fur. Inside, I showed her Bird and she felt my bedcover, opened one or two of my word boxes, had a sniff at the curtains, then went across to Walter who, in one hand, was cradling the apple that had been on the sideboard. There was the smell of ironing and pine from a container. Brandishing a pencil, Walter bumped his head against a window he hadn't seen, the pencil fell from his hand, he must've thought the glass was missing and that that should be mentioned in his report. He rubbed the mark on his forehead, wiped the beads of sweat off and, with a nod, accepted the water my mother put down for him.

He nodded at everything. That's all that one's fit for, my father whispered. He's like a lamb, despite those paws of his. Like a vice, they are. That one can pulverize raw potatoes with one hand, he said, not without envy.

When my mother showed them the cupboards and said to go ahead and open them, Ruth declined, said there's no need to bother, and the two of them listened really closely though my mother didn't say much more and I said even less. Walter wrote it all down, he was sweating, he was soaking wet, and I was sweating like Walter, a bit—I liked him a bit.

Ruth noted there were too few vitamins in the house. My mother took her into the garden again where, at that very moment, vitamins were peeking out of the ground and Walter wrote down the recipe for a diet supplement that would help me to grow and keep my head on course.

Ever since Ruth and Walter had been coming, my mother cleaned the windows in the tomato house too. Even on the inside, you could see them sparkle. They didn't sit down on their next visit, either—they never sat down but wandered round the flat. If they weren't so pushed for time, they drank a coffee standing up, let their eyes do the walking, and Walter nodded and nodded and nodded. Or scratched his head cos—despite all the salad, fresh vitamins and the diet supplement—I wasn't growing. He looked up a table to see what size I'd been when I was delivered and compared that with the tape measure he pulled out bang in front of me.

Blue eyes. Walter had blue eyes. Almost as blue as the sky where Tat lived when the sun was shining, almost as blue as the Rhone Glacier, as lakes like the Blausee and Klöntalersee where we'd taken the woman downstairs for some fresh air and to get some colour in her cheeks, as blue as the blue of the sea in Madame Jelisaweta's pictures of Yugoslavia on the wall of her salon, as blue as bathwater with bathing salts in it, and as blue as the wet Ajax powder my mother used to get the bathroom clean before Ruth and Walter arrived, light blue like Toni's nicest shirt, as light blue as Long-Distance Werner's car, as blue as the air when Eli skipped work sometimes.

Shaking his head, Walter noted the figure in the *records*. People like me need *records* so we can be seen. My *records*, like all records, begin at the beginning, Walter and Ruth said, and are open-ended at the back. Such records, Ruth said, are actually *lists*. Walter sighed and nodded and asked for more water.

Walter, who every time took longer to say goodbye, every time drank more water, every time did so more slowly, who was always re-ordering his notes, who lost his pencil and had to look for it, who—puffing—went back round the flat again, shouted 'There it is!', then looked for his briefcase, discovered he'd not noted something, dabbed his brow, then licked his pencil and was grinding his jaws as he wrote, cleared his throat to say goodbye again, then tapped his briefcase to assure himself he'd everything with him while Ruth walked up and down at the front door and my father whispered, 'Raw potatoes! Telling you—that one can pulverize raw potatoes with one hand.'

Then the door clicked shut, my mother turned the light off and only Ruth's apple smell remained.

We lay down on the sofa. The room dissolved into colours, blue and red and orange, light was coming in all the windows, each lamp had a halo, the edges of things blurred, and the kitchen clock was ticking loudly, as it always did when I took my glasses off. I turned to my mother. She was looking up at the ceiling.

'Am I still growing?'

'Hm?'

'Am I still growing?'

'You're going to be really big one day.' And we're not inviting those two to my funeral. Not Ruth, and not Walter either.'

THE GARDEN'S NOT FOR SISSIES as it's not always crowned with success. It needs lots of rain, lots of sun, all at the right time and in the right amounts. You need good luck, my father said. Last autumn he'd none, he had to plough it all under. Eli said he'd learnt more of our swear words in those two days, than in the past five years on building sites. My father could relax in the garden nevertheless. He liked reaching into the soil, pulling stones and roots out and throwing pebbles at Oskar who wouldn't stop barking in the next garden. He broke up the soil in record time, had asked me to time him on the stopwatch, and when, humming away to himself, he spread the chicken manure on the pumpkins, it looked as if he was seasoning them.

Seeds and kernels were drying on the windowsill. Tearing the windows open was forbidden because then, as well as the pumpkins and apples, the tomatoes, cucumbers and courgettes would go flying and the future vegetables would be scattered round the neighbouring gardens where, with my father watching, they would wither and go bad. My mother rolled her eyes: 'I'm being careful.'

'The sun will bring it to light.'

THE SUN BROUGHT IT TO LIGHT. He darted out of his camp chair, screaming:

'I'll make mincemeat of that dog. Look at that!'

Oskar was peeing against a tomato plant that must've flown over the fence and was now big enough for Oskar to notice. My father turned to my mother.

'That's one of my tomatoes! And why? Because you're a fresh-air fanatic. Because you're a fresh-air fanatic, I can admire my tomatoes all round the neighbourhood. My nose is up against fences so much, it's getting flat. Who, apart from me, grows Ochsenherz tomatoes? And that fleabag is pissing against the plant. It's all the same to him where he pisses. Look! The plant's turning yellow. It's dying.'

As if to order, a few of the little green tomatoes trickled to the ground and Oskar sniffed at them, curiously.

'I don't believe it! Oskar, out!'

My father's hands went up to his face and he fell back on the camp chair. It was a miracle it didn't collapse. He jumped down my throat:

'What are *you* looking at? Go and get me a beer. For God's sake, not even tomatoes get to turn out right in this country! You can hardly peek out of the ground before someone pisses in your face.'

Oskar and the stray tomatoes weren't the only thing that rankled with my father. All kinds of things tried to get at his vegetables—too much rain, too much sun, caterpillars and ants, lice and snails. They squirmed on the blue granules he scattered generously, foaming and forming a pulp that the rain washed away. The lice he banished with a smelly nettle soup that, two weeks later, tiny worms twitched in. He threw it over lettuce thieves too. He had a solution for everything. It was just the mildew that couldn't be defeated. Four of us were in the garden.

'If the sun's the problem, you can water the plants, in the morning and evening. The rain, you can curse. At some point, it will stop. Woe betide you though, if the air remains too damp. Mildew. And you can't get rid of it.'

'Can you write *mildew* down for me?'

'It's time you learnt how to write.'

'We've already done from A to D. Tomorrow, we're doing an E. The teacher promised.'

Eli measured me against his spade and, with a stone, made a notch in the handle. Toni wiped his hands on his trousers and stroked my head.

'She's a bit small for her age.'

'That's what the authorities are saying too. I don't set much store by it. What do they know about growing things? She'll grow in her own time.'

My father licked the end of his pencil and wrote something down. He shook his head.

'There's no cure for mildew. It's as simple as that. My tooth's getting worse, into the bargain.'

Leaning against Snow White's hutch, he opened his mouth and asked us to look into it.

'Which one is it?'

'They all hurt.'

Toni poked round with his finger till my father let out a yell.

'Leave me alone.'

'Cloves. You should chew on a clove.'

MILDEW, I PUT IN MY ILLNESSES BOX, together with FLU, CANCER, HELLISH MISERY, TOOTHACHE and LOVESICK.

CLOVES was going into the FLOWERS box but my father shook his head. He pointed to the SPICES box, then said 'Both, in a way.' He put a few in his mouth. Because he didn't feel like writing, CLO was now in FLOWERS, and VES in SPICES. That evening, he brought a tiny new box into my room. One just for CLOVES. He'd already labelled it.

'What have you written on it?'

'UNIQUE. Might Toni have a great cure for mildew too?'

BECAUSE THEY GOT ON SO WELL, speaking Italian in the garden, my father brought Toni home with him. They traded vegetables. My mother left them, unused, in the fridge till she could wipe them out with a cloth. She couldn't stand Toni. He too had hellish misery, and my mother was in no hurry to catch it. She'd her own already. And definitely didn't like olives.

'That from down there?'

She pointed at the jar he'd put on the table.

'From my home village, yes. The fire left just two trees standing. Of the whole grove, just two trees.'

Turning the jar in his hands, he looked at the table and said that sometimes, deep inside, abroad was nothing but an abyss.

'I know what abroad is like—me.'

She was a globetrotter when it came to things like this. My mother already had her ashes being scattered in the Caribbean when she died. And Errol Flynn sending flowers.

SWITZERLAND HAS PLANS. And one thing was sure—Eli wasn't part of the mix. Concrete was the one thing he got to mix. The wall he was looking up at was at an awkward stage, and his foreman was too. Eli had to get a move on. He was tugging impatiently at the plastic sheet he was spreading out on the ground.

'Go home.'

'I can't.'

'Porque? Why not?'

At home, domestic bliss wasn't what it should be. The Peroxide Blonde said you could hear it down on the street even. Switzerland had plans that were totally upsetting my father. He was banging doors and my mother was going round after him, closing the windows my father had just opened. This had been going on for days already.

'Why are they doing that?'

Eli held a shovel out to me.

'Hold that.'

'Go on, tell me.'

'Because they're not of the same opinion.'

'My father says Switzerland has plans.'

'Plans? What kind of plans?'

'You'll have to explain that to me. The Peroxide Blonde won't tell me anything, says she doesn't understand *politics*. What's *politics*?'

'I haven't time for that right now. As you can see.'

He pointed at a pile of sacks of cement. Eli took one, swung it onto his back using just one hand—none of the other men could do that—and when he dropped it on the ground beside me, the sack burst and we stood in a cloud of dust that only slowly settled again. Eli took the shovel back.

'What do you not look like?!'

'What about *politics*?'

'Give me peace with that. I've enough bother as it is.'

'But it's important. Because of the *referendum*. What's a *referendum*? What's an *initiative*? And what's *foreign infiltration*? I'm not allowed to say that word at home, my father's already smashed the radio cos of it. Now we've no radio and our doors aren't going to last much longer, the Peroxide Blonde says. If we keep on like that, she says, the house will collapse too. My mother doesn't care though. She wants to drive off with me anyhow. Says she can't live with a marriage that's broken, and not with a *democracy* that's broken either, she can't even speak her mind at home. What is *democracy* and what is *politics*?'

You have to remain stubborn if you want something in this country, Eli had said it himself, and especially if you're not sure you can stay. There's agreement across the world on this. Ask anyone who isn't a tourist but making a mad dash for another country cos, back home, they were scared shitless for as many different reasons as Oskar has hairs, Eli says. Him and his pals could tell you a thing or two about that, they could.

'But what about Switzerland, and what's *politics*?'

Eli sighed. He made a hollow in the cement, put the shovel down and pulled me behind the toilet hut that was wobbling and flushing once a minute. It was their break.

'Switzerland is asking itself how many foreigners it wants to have here. Or rather, James Schwarzenbach is asking the Swiss that. There are too many of us, Schwarzenbach reckons.'

'Who is Schwarzenbach? They're talking about him. Everyone is. My mother, Toni—and my father's nose goes white with rage if he even thinks of him. He says Schwarzenbach is completely destroying Switzerland and ruining his marriage. He says Schwarzenbach is a professional arsonist but make out he's a fireman.'

'He's a politician. He wants Switzerland to have a referendum on how many foreigners can be in Switzerland, how many of us can stay.'

'What's *initiative*? And what's *foreign infiltration*?'

'I've just told you.'

'No, you haven't. And not *politics*, and not *democracy*.'

'Your grandfather anyhow says, I've heard, that *democracy* isn't a question of taste or something you can use to make you yourself seem important, even if people like Schwarzenbach like to think so.'

Eli looked to see where his foreman was. He bent down to the shovel, scratched a little dirt together, then mushed it in a puddle to make some browny-grey stuff.

It was starting to rain. He put his collar up, put mine up too and brushed the wet hair out of my face.

'On you go home. I'll see you later.'

THERE ARE WORDS THAT THE FATTEST ENCYCLOPAEDIA beside my bed tells you things about, that tell you nothing. Experience teaches you that.

It was raining pasta and goulash sauce even before the plate hit the wall. My father was even more furious than the Housemother's dog used to get every time the postman who had once fed it barbed-wire sausage showed up. Something in the newspaper had enraged my father and my mother was working him up to livid. They had an *issue*.

Issue: something I wasn't asked about. ISSUE was in the future-words box. I didn't have an ISSUE yet. I merely was one, again and again, just not at this moment. Now, it's James Schwarzenbach, my father or my mother. Depending. It's *a matter of opinion*.

A matter of opinion: not an issue for me either.

Issues are words that foreigners have round their necks, and what's far worse, my mother says, we have the foreigners round our necks cos there are so many of them now, with their suitcases from Italy, word has spread about Switzerland, and my father says Schwarzenbach says that's the reason for the *foreign infiltration* here, *foreign infiltration* is the reason for his *initiative*, and because that was successful, there's now *The Referendum*. I phoned Tat so he could explain the words to me but he didn't listen at all, just roared right away into the receiver that *initiatives* and *referenda* were gradually deteriorating into the favourite sports of *image-obsessed hooligans on the right* and were also contributing to the Swiss expressing their views through the *ballot box*, instead of thinking first about *politics* and the *repercussions*. The rest of what he said, I couldn't understand, and he hung up, no doubt because his false teeth had fallen out again. I decided to think about *politics* immediately—as soon as someone could tell me what it is.

If my father could, he says, he'd run back and forward and vote as often as possible against this Schwarzenbach guy, who is to blame for everything—for my father having to shout, for him having to sleep for the past week on the sofa, for him not being able to sleep on the sofa, for him having to drink cos he's not allowed to sleep in his own bed, for him not being able to find the sofa cos he's been drinking, for him having to sleep on the kitchen floor and not being able to sleep there either, not for a minute.

'1970!' he roars through the kitchen. 'Don't ever forget 1970! This little son-of-an-industrialist. A millionaire who claims to be one of us. Someone who has never lifted a finger, never had to work in his life, whose head it has never entered to work—someone like that's claiming to represent our interests. How can he know what they are? Come on, tell me! Cos if this twerp gets his proposal through, Eli and Toni will have to go home, Dejan and

Mirela will have to go home, and you can stick your red-pepper relish and sheep's cheese and milk bread and all the rest—three hundred thousand foreigners will go back to where they come from, will leave half-finished houses standing and streets dug up, will leave the kitchens, hotels and launderettes where they work, the railway platforms, the foundries, the machine works. Schwarzenbach will be the ruin of them. He's destroying Switzerland, I swear. You don't need a degree to see that. Read up on what the guy wants, read it in his own rag.'

My mother wanted to say something but my father roared he wasn't finished with her yet and certainly not with Schwarzenbach.

'Him and his gang of sympathizers—look at them, they're opening their gobs now, think their chance has come, to do politics. Back then, against Hitler, they clenched their puny little fists in the trouser pocket of their officer uniforms. The other hand was still only interested in business, profit. They weren't actively involved in the war. Certainly didn't help to ensure our borders were closed to those who couldn't afford to pay first the Reich flight tax and then the people smugglers—I defy anyone to tell me otherwise. Having a different opinion was enough to end up on the list of people who would've been shot first. Want to see it? Get Tat to show you next Sunday. His name was on it. The shoemaker in the next village would've fired the shot. A shoemaker! A shoemaker, whose dream it was to make gents' shoes for the industrialists in St Gallen behind all the embroidery.

He was always spineless, him. With those shoes, he'd've been kissing the feet of those predestined to be something or already were something. Whatever! Forget it, after all, it's all history now, right? Now, though, this Schwarzenbach guy's shouting out of every marquee he's invited into that, once again, there are people who have no place here, that they should go, should have to go, and his entourage is making out that anyone who disagrees would be better going too. All this flies in the face of the government's recommendations too. The entire government. It's all in here.'

He waved the newspaper at us, tapped the documents Switzerland had sent out to every household, which my mother was reluctant to read.

'They'll do what they want anyhow.'

'I hope so, in this case.'

'I've nothing to say on the matter. I can't even go and vote yet. So much for the democracy you're vaunting.'

Switzerland doesn't trust just anyone. It picks and chooses. It doesn't trust women, for starters, the Peroxide Blonde had said.

Goulash sauce was dripping from the table, bread lying in the lampshade, pasta smoking on the light bulb. My mother started slowly wiping the wall while my father scratched his head and looked up at the lamp.

'Why, actually, are we having pasta with the goulash?'

'Because we're out of potatoes.'

It was quiet for a while, my mother lit a cigarette and threw her cleaning cloth into a corner.

'This democracy can shove it!'

'The pasta's nearly burning.'

'Then get it down again. And remove the bread from the lampshade while you're at it.'

With the chair in his hand, my father climbed onto the table, swept whatever was lying there together with his foot, then got up on the chair.

'Nonetheless—what kind of a country is it when Schwarzenbach and his consorts can play with the people's fears, make money out of their fears. After a war like that too?!'

'As if you'd any experience of it. The shoemaker didn't shoot. Here, nobody shot, no one was shot or went up in the air, nothing went to pot, no one had to get away from here, everyone stayed at home, no one was trapped in their cellars if, indeed, there were any for people to hide in. No one starved to death anywhere or froze to death or died of fear.'

'Thank God for that! And Tat, Tat was just lucky, more so than Grüninger, you know that as well as I do. Standing at Customs, and—by night—moving people and goods across the Rhine, from Austria into Switzerland. That's precisely why I ask: What kind of a country is it where people applaud those whose opinions play with fire, those to whom the only thing that matters is stoking the flames and who even have the cheek to call that freedom?'

'We have to keep together.'

'Oh yes? What do we have to keep together then? I can gladly tell you—their money. Nothing else. For that, they'll even part with democracy. For that, they'll give democracy a kicking because they don't give a shit about it.'

'There are a lot of foreigners, you've got to admit. They'll end up being too much for us.'

My father, now very quiet, put his glass down slowly.

'Is that right? Let's hope Schwarzenbach and his lot don't get too much for us. You should know why. Hadn't you to get out of France when Hitler was razing it to the ground—in order, supposedly, to liberate it.'

My father swept the broken plate up, then stood up again and threw the shovel and bits of plate at the wall, albeit not the one my mother had just wiped. He screamed that foreign infiltration and idiocy were one and the same and that he couldn't get his head round one thing—why he'd to listen to such idiocy from a woman who was half-French. She spelt out for him what would happen if our Customs collapsed and foreign countries all just flooded into Switzerland. As a Frenchwoman, she didn't want that either, as someone who was half-French, for, after all, she was half-Swiss too. And if there was only Italian food, she'd starve to death with a full plate in front of her—their food's so long, you have to twirl it round your fork. And she'd starve to death anyhow cos there'd be no work for him, wasn't he useless when it came to money? And then the languages—first the Italians and half of Yugoslavia, a bit of Turkey—then it's the Chinese, and before you know it, you're eating ćevapčići with chopsticks.

'What's more—with your ration coupons, in Switzerland, you were able to sleep through the Nazis. But pretend I didn't say anything. It's all over now anyway, finally over, and I really do know what I'm talking about—foreign infiltration isn't idiocy but a fact. It's already starting here in the stairwell. You can smell it.'

Foreign infiltration, *initiative*, *referendum*. Three terms. An *issue*. Not *a matter of opinion*: '*Conviction*,' Eli says.

His sigh is longer than the river we live next to.

WE OFTEN WENT FOR A WALK IN THE TOWN, especially on Sundays, when my father would take us out for a stroll cos it was cheap. My mother also went for walks in town just with me. She said it did me good. Though I didn't notice myself, I trusted her when she said it, as my emotions—as she explained woman to woman once—were a world still to be opened up to me. Sometimes we visited the biggest tree with the best view and then went to the small zoo, to see Almost-No-Feathers. He needed a regular orange. For the vitamins.

For some time now though, my mother hadn't been saying much on these walks. As we strolled, she'd stare into the air and not look at the shop windows. Three times already, I'd shown her the red bike I wanted, and three times she looked at it as if she'd never seen it before. On the bench with the best view, my mother spread the little blanket out and sat down in her nicest flowery dress. She didn't even take the sandwiches out.

'I can't think of anything.'

Then she looked at the sun without blinking. She'd forgotten her sunglasses. I was worried about her, from woman to woman. I got restless, and getting restless always meant trouble for me as I was sure to cause other children problems that would need stitches. The fact we went to the zoo at all after that was a wonder. That's why

I'd made my best moon-eyes at her. Almost-No-Feathers had been waiting on his orange for two weeks already. No doubt he was completely out of vitamins. Ruth would've raised her eyebrows. And Walter would've licked his pencil and written it down.

Right at the back of the cage, Almost-No-Feathers was tampering with the last of his tail feathers. I peeled the orange and held it out to him. It was a good while before he came up to the bars of the cage and reached for the segment of fruit. He dribbled juice, bristled the few remaining feathers on his neck, let me pet him and whistled so loudly, the zookeeper came up and grinned.

'Was there ice-cream for him?'

Almost-No-Feathers and I would've had a lot to say to each other had my mother not been so impatient. She was pacing up and down as if something had stung her and rummaging in her handbag for something.

'Let's drop in on Toni. But where have I my house keys?'

'I have them.'

'Give them to me. The key to Toni's flat is on there too.'

'You've a key to Toni's flat?'

'To see to the flowers.'

'Has Toni flowers?'

'Come on now. We've still to pick up milk too.'

'But I got some yesterday. You told me to. Today's Sunday.'

'Then let's go to Toni's.'

The zookeeper patted me on the shoulder.

'On you go. I'll take care of him.'

He made a few clicking noises, put a finger into the cage and nodded to my mother. Almost-No-Feathers started to purr like a cat and when my mother looked to him for an explanation, the zookeeper shrugged.

'He learnt that from Queequeg, a tomcat we kept in the neighbouring compound for a few months. Years ago now. Washed ashore down at the river, it was. Completely famished and neglected. Totally scared. Claws on it like a big cat. We nursed it back. The bird's been purring ever since.'

'What's its name anyway?'

'Since back then? Ismael. Before that—no idea. I've not been here that long.'

TONI COULD ONLY MAKE SPAGHETTI, salad and sandwiches but his spaghetti were the best and he buttered the bread on which he then piled so much meat, cheese, tomatoes, gherkins, pickles and olives, it was impossible to get it in your mouth.

This time, he put sunflower seeds and a jug of water on the table and brought a big pile of books out of the bedroom.

'Photos from home.'

We sat down on the sofa. My mother on the left, Toni on the right, me in the middle with an album on my knees. I was allowed to touch his dark brown curls. As always on Sundays, he was wearing the light blue shirt that made him look like a film star. He explained the photos in a German I didn't understand very well. Dejan and Mirela didn't speak like that, Eli didn't either, he just rummaged in his pockets sometimes when he was stuck for a word. The corners of the album were cracked and the photos had stains. No wonder—Toni was impatient and would force the pictures out of the mounting corners and walk round with them, come back again, point at everything in them, also at everything that wasn't in them, what was in front of that, behind that, what's different now, what's no longer there, relatives, for example, or the colours. The description of all the colours in black-and-white photos was especially important to him.

Giallo: the yellow of the evening light that was nothing like the yellow in the photo that—in reality—was completely golden. *Oro*, the same word in Italian as in Spanish, and yet there's no comparison. This gold isn't an international gold, it's a personal one, a matter of the heart. And you forgive it for burning during the day, the fact it has the landscape boiling, the air trembling, the fact the air's boiling hot and everyone and everything lies down and sleeps in the early afternoon—the Italians, the Italian dogs, the Italian cats, the Italian flies, the market, the local and the imported trees, the wind that comes from Africa, so hot that everyone has a siesta, is on holiday for a few hours, and all you can hear are the ventilators and the idiots from the hospital with railings round it, and behind it, tomatoes as far as the horizon, nothing but blue above the green and the red. The air, Toni said, calms down only in the evening and brings a wind from Africa again, from another part, he guessed, cos this one wakes the Italians and chases them into the kitchen, onto the roofs and along to the market, to their work and into church.

Blu: he fetched a tin of tomatoes from the kitchen, had a lot of these, now he'd found them in the shopping centre. The blue on the label, he swore, was the blue of the sky at home. And the green on the branches of the tomatoes—a green that *sweats*—was that the word for it?—an aroma—

'*Oozes*.'

'*Oozes* an aroma that tells you who picked it: *verde*.'

Toni could smell green. Green smelt bitter.

'Like the end of a cucumber?'

'More like a spice.'

'And when the sun has gone?'

'At night, the white of cheese. *Mozzarella*. A full moon on your plate and the sound of cicadas.'

How long had we already been sitting in Toni's? For a while he'd not said anything. We were nibbling sunflower seeds and he brushed the salty husks into a big pile. The water jug was empty. Every now and again, he looked at my mother. And I looked at Toni.

The photos were so small, so glossy. When he stuck them back in the album, I was amazed they couldn't sing, they didn't swoosh, didn't toot, didn't laugh, hum or rattle, that no one was sleeping in them or running, that the pictures didn't pollute the air and didn't smell, apart from of the cupboard where they were kept, and of lemon like Toni. Once I was Toni's age, I wanted to smell of lemon too and have curls and wear light blue shirts that made me look like a film star. And all week long, not just on a Sunday. I fully intended to. I'd decided already.

'You're going away?'

My mother pointed at the huge suitcase and the three cardboard boxes, all ready to go.

'Yes. Tomorrow already. Much earlier than planned. My mother's not well. Not at all well.'

'Oh.'

'And I need to see how the house is getting on.'

'A house?'

That was of a lot of interest to my mother. There was finally some colour in her face again. My mother thought building houses was great. Houses were coming into fashion.

'Yes, my brother's. He works in Germany. Wants to come home. At some point.'

'And you?'

He shrugged.

'When I'm here, I want back. When I'm in Italy, I want back here. It hasn't been like that for long.'

The flowery dress suited my mother fantastically well. Large, red and pink flowers, a white background.

She'd had her hair cut by Madame Jelisaweta yesterday and now she'd a bit more colour in her face and was smiling a little, she looked like something from an advert for toothpaste, shampoo, lipstick, skin cream, perfume and fashion. Blink, said Tat, blink once, and if I was lucky, the image would remain in my head for ever.

'Spaghetti?'

I nodded.

'Then we can play hide-and-seek.'

'Under the bed included?'

'Under the bed included. But first, I have to make a phone call. It won't take long.'

Ever since he'd moved to Switzerland to work, Toni had horrendously high phone bills. In San Marzano, the telegraph wires were smoking above the tomatoes and shuddering in the wind, he said, and here, the bills can hardly fit through the slit in the mailbox. Toni was a have-not too, my father said. Like us. Almost. He has nothing you'd want to steal, the postman said. Every morning, he'd pour plastic into little moulds, and in the afternoon, he'd vet them. In the evenings though, Toni sometimes went to a different factory where he wore thick glasses, several layers of clothes, gloves and an overall, and where, using tongs, he'd to plunge everything they brought to him into a tub.

'What's in there, is something I don't know,' Toni said. 'It breaks up fat, they say, and makes holes in clothes, but it brings good money in. It's not so bad, the galvanizing plant. A good factory. Good people. My people. Lots of us.'

Once something had fallen from his tongs, it splashed, and his clothes looked afterwards as if Old Shatterhand had fired his Bear Killer at him at least ten times. My mother had been in a complete tizzy, cos of that.

'That's extremely dangerous, terrible. You have to stop doing it.'

As she said it, she was stroking the scraps of cloth like she would Snow White's fur. What if what had happened to Toni had happened to me. If there was the slightest little hole in my trousers, she made a big fuss and threatened to lock my word boxes away for a week. Once I was a film star, I'd pay good money to have holes made in my clothes. I intended to do that too.

'THERE'S SOMETHING NOT RIGHT WITH TONI,' my father said.

'He's Italian,' my mother said.

When he was drinking a beer with Eli out at the hutch, my father was still surprised at my mother's answer but pleased about something he called her *change of heart*. Eli said the referendum had turned out well, but only just. Fifty-four to forty-six—in percentage terms, a narrow result.

'What's a *change of heart*?'

'Something you don't need to know about yet.'

'Don't be like that.'

Eli nudged my father in the side.

'Eli, what's *percentage terms*? Will you write it down for me?'

Eli wrote down: *percentage terms*, and my father opened another bottle of beer, it had a percentage too, he said. Eli treated my father to so many percentages, he'd to sleep on the sofa again, and it took my mother ages to calm down. No doubt, domestic bliss wasn't what it should be, again. And you could hear it down on the street.

I put PERCENTAGE TERMS down on the table. Whether in a referendum or beer, these percentage things caused problems. And no way did my father want a word box for PROBLEMS. At best, he could've imagined it in the workshop or garage. He certainly didn't want it staring him in the face.

FOUR ORANGES HAD ROTTED AWAY in the time we'd not been to the zoo. My mother had thrown each one away when it started to smell and attract flies. Rotten oranges weren't a good idea for two reasons—Ruth and Walter. Stale air, flies and fly shit were all bad news. A hellish misery like my mother currently had would make the worst possible impression. She burst into tears for no reason. I thought of Almost-No-Feathers, burst into tears too, and my father put his hands over his face, banged doors like before a referendum and went out into the garden. Then all was quiet.

'Can't we go to Almost-No-Feathers and to the biggest tree with the nicest view?'

No answer.

'Can I open the curtains?'

No answer.

'Do you want your pills?'

Outside, my father turned the lawnmower on. I fetched the torch and, using my paintbox, took my own fingerprints. Eli had said they were clear proof of who you were and the police swore by them. My mother listened for an hour to Oskar barking at my father's lawnmower. Only when the postman wouldn't stop ringing did she give herself a push.

In the toilet, it's quiet. You can think your thoughts without being disturbed. I waited outside, to help my mother a bit.

'What you doing?'

'Freshening myself up.'

When she came out, it was like a sub had come on. She tore open the curtains and windows.

'My goodness, how stuffy it is in here.'

She smelt of flowers, drank a glass of water and turned round to me.

'What do you not look like?'

She dampened her comb and smoothed my hair down.

'Get dressed.'

'Where we going?'

'To the zoo. I'll take you there, and come and fetch you later. OK?'

I nodded. The letter that had helped to freshen her up, she put in her pocket.

'HAVE YOU BEEN WAITING HERE LONG?'

The zookeeper wasn't moving from the spot.

'Where's your mother?'

With his neck up against the bars, Almost-No-Feathers was cracking and purring constantly. Non-stop, like a teleprinter. He stuck a foot out and reached for my finger.

'Isn't it your mother you always come with?'

The zookeeper stopped for a moment.

'Are you not talking to me? Is she well?'

'She's OK.'

'We're closing soon.'

'She's in the toilet. She's coming to fetch me.'

'But there's no one there. I've just been.'

'She's not in the Gents.'

'We check both when we're about to close. There's no one there. And it's getting dark.'

It was indeed. It was almost dark. The lights were on. Doors creaked here and there.

'Will you come with me?'

'I'm not allowed to go anywhere with anyone. She's fetching me here.'

'Come on, I'll take you home.'

He took me by the hand and led me past the pay booth. Another zookeeper was locking the entrance to the zoo. He tapped his hat with one finger. In the big room I was taken to, a fat man was lighting a pipe. He looked a bit like Walter. He drank a full glass of water, poured some more, then looked at me from head to toe.

'What's your name?'

A huge cloud of smoke floated past me. The man rocked back in his chair.

'Where do you live?'

The leather squeaked, it was quiet for a while, then he said through the fumes:

'Oh, OK then. My name is Dr Gábor. You can call me Gabesz. You like Ismael, I hear. Come on, tell us, where do you belong?'

Not even Ruth and Walter could've told him that. They were still working on my records. The man stroked his arm.

'Who can I phone for you?'

The Housemother used to stroke her arm too, she would stroke our hair, stroke her dog, stroke the fur of living rabbits and of dead ones before Helene skinned them, she'd even stroke the skin of the fish before Helene lifted them out of the bucket to clobber them.

'Who should I phone?'

'The Housemother.'

'The Housemother. Fine. And where can I find her?'

I told him the address.

'Oh, that's where you're from. So you've run away.'

CARS WERE PARKING IN THE STREET, the bus stopped and moved off again, a lorry was turning at the bus stop, and in my room, the lights were wandering round the walls. My suitcase was gleaming in the corner. It wasn't even half the size of Toni's.

'A thousand deaths,' said Eli. 'Sometimes you die a thousand deaths.'

I closed my eyes. It didn't help. Colour blurred into the blackness. It wasn't possible to see *nothing*.

My father pulled the cover away from over my face. His nose was white as snow.

'You two had a quarrel.'

'It's OK now.'

'Where's Toni?'

'Upstairs. Upstairs, of course.'

'Where's she?'

'Next door.'

'Does she no longer want me? Do I have to go back?'

'Back where?'

'To the Housemother.'

'What gave you that idea? She was amazed by the phone call.'

'Why did she keep me waiting so long?'

I pointed through to next door. He clicked his tongue. It took ages before he came out with it.

'That's what she said?'

'Yes.'

'She misplaced me?'

'Something like that. She hides things that are especially valuable well. So well, not even she knows any more where they are.'

'Why?'

'They're then safe. There.'

'A thousand deaths,' says Eli. 'Sometimes you die a thousand deaths.'

Tears, lots of tears. Lágrimas. Eli gives me words too. Muchas lágrimas into your pillow, and it's sure to come, sleep, el sueño. I'm waiting.

WORDS WERE BILLOWING OUT of all the boxes, they flew across the room when my mother opened the windows. They were a thorn in her flesh. She threatened to throw away all the words and all the boxes if I didn't tidy them up. Those in the tins too, which were piling up on the windowsill—hardy words. Tat called them that. The ones from early childhood, they can take anything.

But I couldn't tidy up. The words were constantly changing boxes, from BEFORE to NOW and from NOW to BEFORE, from BEFORE to LATER, and there are more and more in LATER, and in BEFORE too, whereas NOW ran out on me, and there were words that belonged nowhere, not even in your mouth. I was getting on everyone's nerves and yet *puberty*, the thing my mother feared as much as big bills, hadn't broken out in me yet.

That I was getting on everyone's nerves, I knew from my mother. It's called *socialization*. It's beginning now, is finally taking hold, Ruth and Walter said. They reassured my mother it would still be a while until *puberty* started but my mother wasn't to be reassured. She cried at the kitchen table, worse than any time she'd had hellish misery.

'Have you gone completely mad? Do you realize Imelda's head needed nine stitches? Hitting someone with a shovel—what were you thinking? Why with a shovel?'

'She messed with me.'

'I'm about to mess with you.'

She shot up, her hands went up to her head, she asked herself where my father had got to, he should have a word with Imelda too—Imelda who, at the moment, is saying absolutely nothing, is just pale and has a bald head and is lying in hospital cos of her sore head.

I could've read pages and pages to her, right away, from the Encyclopaedia of Good Reasons that Tat and I continued to write every Sunday and filled with ISSUES and ARGUMENTS, but my mother didn't look as if she wanted to hear a single word even. Though it was already over a thousand pages long, she'd have shot it down in flames, simply. Her way with words gives her the strength of ten demolition balls, Eli said.

'We're going to go to the hospital now and you're going to apologize.'

'I can't.'

'Not half, you can.'

ALL HER HAIR WAS OFF, IMELDA WAS BALDER than Almost-No-Feathers. Her skull was throbbing, as if something wanted out. In the seam where the skin was sewn together stretched black thread.

Shuffling, whispering, as we arrived. The curtain was open a bit. I should've apologized.

I couldn't do it.

Imelda was sleeping after the operation, she was in a deep sleep, was sleeping longer than her mother would've wanted, was holding a bloody cloth in her hand. And *I* might not have wanted to open my mouth but there were all kinds of things *she* wanted to say. She wanted to speak. About Imelda's head and the hole in it and about her knowing what should happen to me. She held the bloody cloth out to my mother, told us to have a look at that, a good look at that, we should then take a hike and I could get to hell or even better—back where I came from. She wished my mother good luck with me and threw the cloth after us. For the whole journey back, my mother folded and re-folded it into ever-smaller squares, she looked out of the window without saying a word and, at home, put it down on the kitchen table and roared, 'Sit down!'

We didn't move from the spot until my father came. He looked first at the cloth on the table, then at us.

'What's that?'

'Your daughter was in a fight. No, actually, she wasn't even in a fight, she hit out at someone. With a cement shovel. She split Imelda's head, nearly, with a shovel. Imelda's in hospital.'

'And what else?'

'And what else? She's sleeping, she's unconscious, I've no idea. They haven't phoned. Her mother threw us out.'

I crawled under the kitchen table and could hear my mother say, 'She threw us out because the little one doesn't even think an apology's necessary.'

My father paced up and down quickly, stopping now and then to gulp some beer. He bent down.

'You'll apologize!' he shouted. 'And sit at the table like a decent person.'

I said nothing and sat down.

'Nine stitches,' my mother said.

'But they—'

'None of your stories now.'

'Nine stitches,' my mother said. 'Nine. Her glasses are broken too.'

The whole time already, I'd been fingering the cracked glass. All that could be heard now were my father's footsteps, the hiss of the beer bottle, the hiss of a second, tops falling and spinning on the tiled floor, the glass that—with a crack and in star-shaped pieces—came away from the frame, and the clout that came from nowhere. I fell off the chair. Before my eyes, blurs of colour. The noise, razor-sharp.

'Scram. Just go.'

THE BED. THE TABLE. WORD BOXES. The shelf. Books. Word boxes. The street. Its light. The lamp, its light. Light off.

A shovel in her head. Imelda. And Natural Disaster.

BENT OVER A TREASURE MAP, I imagine all the things that could be in the chest I've drawn, using brown and yellow. Cos there's no gold. You only get that in the big boxes of crayons and they're out of the question cos gold and silver get stolen, the big ones would trade them for cigarettes. Mix yellow and brown and you don't get gold, just some kind of muck on the page. The door opens and the Housemother comes in, claps her hands and shouts:

'There's cake in an hour. Meet in the kitchen. Call and tell the others.'

The Housemother gives us an hour's warning always, so we can look like human beings, so we're fit to appear before her, so the brown and yellow can be washed off our hands, chewing gum can be removed from people's hair, tidemarks from wherever she might find them, so a plaster can be put on any cut that has been scratched open again, so she gets to see something that smells good, has been ironed properly and holds out a hand she won't immediately catch some terrible illness from. And then this happens: I fall flat on my face, nearly, with shock—and it's not just me, cos on the table are cakes that beat everything Helene ever baked, not even on the Housemother's milestone birthday was there anything like that. Pink cakes, white or full of chocolate, with Smarties on top, or carrots made of marzipan, and Martin shouts, just like that, they looked just like that when they re-married, and you never believed me, whipped cream, three storeys high, and you never believed me, and now look.

The Housemother wants us to button our lips, says we've been given them as a gift, by someone we don't know, we can't even thank the benefactor.

Now we finally have to believe this kind of thing exists, Martin can't calm down, he's enjoying his triumph, says, all this, this is tremendous, not at all bad in actual fact, really quite nice, but still no comparison to his parents' wedding cakes, and while we tie our napkins round our necks and join the queue, the mountains of cake at his parents' second wedding get higher and higher, they're touching the ceiling already, and for the biggest one, his parents need a ladder. Donelli—who is short—says, rightly, oh come off it, they could no longer have got up a ladder, they were too drunk already after the first hour.

No doubt, it's about to kick off again, Martin will ruin the party, throw cake everywhere instead of eating it, will grab hold of something and hit it, and we'll all have to leave, will want to leave, despite the cake will want nothing more, but he doesn't say a word, just joins the queue, and then a second time, and then he helps himself, eats until he turns yellow and then white and then races out of the kitchen and the Housemother has to make sure he's OK.

Things got more serious than we thought. She fetched the doctor. The first time he could go to the toilet alone again, he soiled his pants in front of us. Brown stuff ran out of his pyjamas that stank as far as the kitchen. We held our noses. No one touched him as he lay there, all skin and bone and covered in shit, on the tiles. We did nothing to hold him up or help him up, we let him crawl, stood round him, everyone keeping the exact same distance, followed him, nipping one another and holding our breaths when holding on to a door handle, he tried to straighten up. Sniggering, we watched as he caved in again and again, as his trousers and vest got stained, and he crawled along the floor towards the toilet, leaving a trail our whispers commented on.

It was the silence that attracted the Housemother's attention. She gave whoever was closest a clout, shook her head, said we were to pull ourselves together, this was a natural disaster, just, and we were all to get away. Getting a name that bore no relation to the one you were christened with, didn't take long—it took all the longer to get rid of it again. Later, the little ones called him Bog-Hogger and got battered for it. For me, he remained Natural Disaster.

He didn't just hit you with the palm of his hand or his fist. No, he filled sand into the little sack we'd been given on St Nicholas Day and thrashed us until we puked. He put stones in snowballs that he dipped in water, then left out on the windowsill overnight. The next day, he'd cradle them in his hand and just look at us. He made a sport of waiting—ages—before he threw them. He hit everyone, he shoved everyone down the toilet that he blocked and then let overflow. He could get so furious, even the oldest children couldn't get hold of him, not even four of them could hold him. If you laughed, you got thumped. If you didn't laugh, he gave you a slap. And things got really bad if you mentioned Uncle Eugen. It was enough to say Uncle Eugen must've forgotten him and to raise your eyebrows. He'd burnt Johann at the stake for that. He stood over him until the rubber of his boots started blistering. Only then did he pour water over him and warn us not to untie him. It was snowing constantly. Steam came off Johann—who was lashed onto the stake—for half an hour. If Natural Disaster hadn't stuffed a cloth in his mouth, you'd have heard his teeth chattering as far away as the edge of the forest. No one untied him, we'd had to swear on our lives we wouldn't, lives that didn't matter a shit to Natural Disaster—as he swore to us. Just think of what happened to Johann, he said. Of course, we thought of what was happening to Johann, we couldn't think of anything but Johann, not the whole day, not at supper either, even if it was our favourite meal, elbow macaroni with mince and stewed apple. But who felt like eating? Natural Disaster was eating for two, stuffing himself, he kept an eye on us, spread himself out at the table so no one noticed Johann was missing. Johann's plate, he had on his lap, and even before we got as far as the pear there was for dessert, we could stand it no longer and crept to Johann and took the cloth out of his mouth and crawled away again. Johann screamed the place down.

Natural Disaster was given another chance. He had a history. We all had a history, I'd one too. Not having one counted as one, was something, at least, that made people wonder. That's why I was here, whether I had one or not. Natural Disaster had enough history for at least two people, he made up for those who didn't have one, which was several of us. The Housemother was stuck with him. Martin's mountain of files, she said, is something no one wants to climb. Apart from Helene. She didn't give up.

If we got up to no good, Helene always dragged us out into Nature behind the house. We'd to watch the vegetables grow.

'Vegetables don't have to be told what to do. Take the potato. It knows itself what to do, you don't have to tell it first,' she said. 'It's just you lot that are too stupid, more stupid than any potato. Kindly take a leaf out of the lettuce's book! And the cauliflower's! And the tomatoes!'

Natural Disaster spent whole afternoons trying to learn from the vegetables. But he would nod off and miss everything. In the evening, he'd come back in, well rested, and take his room apart cos he was looking for something. All year, Helene would shake her head if ever anyone mentioned it. She was at her wit's end with Natural Disaster, Professor of Growing Vegetables or not.

Natural Disaster got hold of me one day in the apple orchard. Or rather, I caught him doing something and he bent down and put his finger to his lips after hitting me with a hoe. Next thing, I was out for the count. Helene found me. She bit her lips, just like she did when the priest came and the first thing he did was kick the dog. She called the gardener. The gardener called the

Housemother, the Housemother the doctor. He looked at the wound, wanted to know what my name was, what the Housemother's name was. At first, it refused to come to mind and he muttered that Natural Disaster was well on the way to making a name for himself.

They shook their heads.

'And yet he has everything he needs.'

Natural Disaster had everything it takes to go quickly. He had eyes women would later dream of, the Housemother and fat Helene agreed. He'd an immaculate set of teeth he could crack nuts with—a gap that, without exception, everyone found sweet. And he had curls. Helene called his hair a magnificent head of curls, even the gardener had to agree with her on that. Apart from once, he'd never been ill, he always looked fresh. Whether he'd had to help in the garden or the workshop or he'd been in a fight, he always managed to get his hands clean again.

The Housemother examined potential clients very carefully, as far as their financial possibilities were concerned and their reputation was.

She visited clients at home and, sometimes, the clients' neighbours. She asked the police whether the clients had a clean slate. If they did, she invited them for coffee, so they could have a look round and see did anything appeal. They always came in pairs. At the front door already, they'd stumble upon Natural Disaster and be very impressed. They'd want to know his name. They'd look at each other, look at the Housemother, repeat the name as if she were Santa Claus. They'd look round as if looking for something and look at Natural Disaster as if they'd found it.

'He's cute,' they'd say.

I'd have liked to tell them that Natural Disaster was anything but cute. That he hangs around the door only cos he thinks Uncle Eugen is going to turn up to fetch him. That he can't help his eyes, that he's not looking to go with them, that he'd only go cos he has to, cos he has to go for a while so the Housemother can have a holiday from him, so we can all have a holiday from him, cos if he were to come back, if they were to bring him back, they'd be the ones needing a holiday. We, though, would've recovered enough to cope with Natural Disaster again and the ideas that come to him with a fury. A fury that borders on madness, as the shrink said, but isn't. And that's why he doesn't have to leave but can stay here, why he definitely can't be taken anywhere else, even if that means bits and pieces getting broken sometimes.

No, I preferred to say nothing and let the clients just get on with it, let them creep round Natural Disaster, let them look at him and go for a walk with him. I went to see the gardener in the apple orchard or sat down on the woodpile until it was over, until he was gone.

Clients could put up with him for at most half as long as they could with me. And quite unlike me, Natural Disaster could remember his original home well. I couldn't get enough when he talked about it.

Whenever his father came home, the police turned up at hourly intervals and over such a long period that eventually Natural Disaster was on first-name terms with them and allowed to call them Uncle Eugen. Uncle Eugen often accompanied his father, together with his pals, home in the box-type van. Leaving him alone on the back seat wasn't an option, a few had to keep a sharp eye on him as his fingers were always itching. At some point, Uncle Eugen stopped preventing his father from throwing the furniture out of the window, or the dishes, so he finally had some order in his life, and could begin again, right from the start. Only if he tried to throw Natural Disaster out after them too—cos his mother couldn't get hold of him—did Uncle Eugen take him with them and Natural Disaster was allowed to sleep in the cell while Uncle Eugen dealt with the paperwork and they'd wake him the next morning with hot chocolate, the best hot chocolate, Natural Disaster said, that he'd ever drunk in his life.

The State didn't like Uncle Eugen occupying a cell almost every night with Natural Disaster. So much public space hadn't been envisaged for Natural Disaster—so, Uncle Eugen had to hand him in to the Housemother. He stood shivering in the hall. They hadn't even taken him home for a change of clothes. Uncle Eugen apologized—he didn't even have a change of clothes there as his father had fallen out a window the night before and his mother was now at an address unknown, together with his bed and the furniture that must still have been there cos his father hadn't got very far with throwing out the furniture, emptying the bathroom cupboard, the kitchen cupboard, the wall units. Only the clothes that had been in the rucksack were lying in the street, cars had driven over them, one had even brushed against his father who was said to have dropped like a stone, quite unlike the clothes that were still sailing down out of the night sky whereas his father was already lying among the smashed-up dishes and foaming bath salts, with the rain pelting down on him—a sad end. Uncle Eugen told him and the Housemother every last detail, as if he was watching a film, as if with his policeman's eye he had to write a report so the Housemother was informed. All of this could be heard from the stairs. Natural Disaster had his hands over his ears and once Uncle Eugen was gone, he spelled out to the Housemother:

'Tomorrow night, I'll be sleeping at Uncle Eugen's in the cell again. He'll be taking me away from here. Uncle Eugen's coming to get me tomorrow.'

That was the first thing he told Donelli too, who shared a room with him.

Uncle Eugen was never seen here again. Natural Disaster cooled his heels at the door in vain, and again and again, someone would admire him for his beautiful eyes, our gardener would see them standing there, from his ladder up against the apple tree, he'd see them holding their hands out towards Natural Disaster, see Natural Disaster standing there, him turning away. And once the gardener shook his head. Climbing down off the ladder, he took two rungs at once. It was already almost dark and you could see his breath. He pointed at the sky. He was keen on stars, knew almost all their names.

'The scientists go to some trouble with the names,' he said, 'they've some imagination, they call half-stars that don't make it to more than a cloud of gas, that fail to form properly, that don't have the strength, that can never become a whole star and shine down as far as us—they call these half-stars "brown dwarfs", that's their name. They're the failures of the universe, they say, and they're so far away, we can't know whether we're right about what we say about them. But not even a fly can live on them.'

BEFORE MY FATHER LEFT THE HOUSE the next day, he put a big box on the table. Even without my glasses, I could see it.

'For me?'

He nodded. The cardboard box was so big I couldn't get both arms round it. I pulled it over. It was light. My heart was beating as I opened it.

'There's nothing in it.'

'Not yet. It's for you to start collecting.'

'What?'

With a thick felt pen, and spelling the word out loud, he wrote on the lid: A-POL-OG-IES.

'And give the best one to Imelda.'

He bent down so I could see him clearly.

'The very best one.'

He put a small bag down beside it.

'For your glasses.'

He brushed up the bits of the glasses on the table, made a small pile, right beside my hand.

'Where's the other side?'

'Don't know.'

'What do you mean, don't know? Go and get it.'

His voice was already furious again, as furious as yesterday, I didn't look at him, my eyes were too watery, the water, about to overflow, would wash the pattern, the grapes and apples, out of the tablecloth. The pattern had been constantly changing shape all morning, the fruits getting liquidy and wiggling across the table, together with the stars and the rainbows—my father, a big blob that cast a shadow. I blinked and slipped down off the chair.

My father was no longer there when I came back. I put the other side of the glasses on the table and tried to look nowhere.

With my glasses in bits in a little bag, my mother and I went into town.

At the optician's, I put the bag down on the table. He whistled through his teeth.

'Those really are beyond repair. So let's see.'

His shoes crunched as he disappeared into another room. He came back with a handful of glasses.

He asked me to look through an instrument and tell him what way the letters were pointing. But there was nothing but two blobs. The optician raised his eyebrows and said there was a new way of making thick glasses thinner, with a slim silhouette. But my mother wanted the thickest cos they're the cheapest, and a steel frame because they're eternal, will survive a car accident, and are as supple as a skyscraper, so ready for an earthquake.

'What's *silhouette*?'

I wasn't given an answer. The optician mentioned *silhouette* again, and *beautiful design*, and I asked:

'What's *silhouette*?'

He looked at my mother and I looked at him.

'How expensive is it?'

It was so expensive that on the way home, she told me there'd be no ice-cream for three weeks, TV was banned already, the gun and the cowboy hat, listening to the radio, the bow and arrow, and visits to Almost-No-Feathers too. I wouldn't have any time for all that anyway cos I'd to go to the hospital and tell Imelda I was sorry. As soon as she was able to hear me again.

'I'll take you.'

Imelda wasn't able to hear me all day long. By hitting her, I'd put a *coma* in her head. While the doctors had been able to sew the *coma*, they now had to observe it, and they were able to do that best if Imelda stayed still, just slept and said nothing. Imelda said nothing to me, Imelda said nothing to the nurses, the doctors, her father and her mother, who cried when she wasn't speaking to Imelda but reaching for the tube that led to her arm, who rang for the nurses, spoke to the doctors and did some *plain-talking* to me. Imelda's doctor read me *the riot act*. Imelda's mother's *plain-talking* gave me a sore tummy. And I got diarrhoea from the doctor's *riot act*. I put COMA, PLAIN-TALKING and RIOT ACT in the word box for ILLNESSES. The big APOLOGIES box remained empty.

The next day, my new glasses were ready and Imelda got to wake up, the doctors let her. My mother cried together with Imelda's mother, a nurse brought cake and, to mark the occasion, I got to hear what *silhouette* means.

Silhouette: makes you happy and your heart beat (Eli).

Silhouette: oh, you mean *THE Silhouettes*. Their music was very good. They were around until not so long ago (my father).

Silhouette: something the Peroxide Blonde is battling with (my mother).

Tat didn't want to say anything on the subject, he just asked on the phone, 'Have you apologized to Imelda yet?'

I shook my head. He slurped some coffee from his saucer, I could hear it.

'You'll have to go over the Encyclopaedia of Good Reasons again. She could've died.'

DUST WAS MAKING MY SKIN ITCH, clouds of it were hanging in the light. It was grey, whitish grey, on my glasses. We were in the workshop. The new chair for Tat was nearly ready. My father was doing the final touches. I was sitting in a dense fog, as if I'd forgotten to put my glasses on, but no matter how thick it got, my thoughts remained as red as Imelda's scar.

Her hair was still gone. It was in no hurry to grow. Fluff, dragging its feet. No one could comfort the hair, no one knew how.

She could've died, Madame Jelisaweta had said too.

'What does Death look like?'

'Different for each person,' my father answered.

'There's not just one?'

'No.'

'You've one all for yourself?'

'In a way.'

'Will you show me him?'

'I can't.'

'Why not?'

'Because he isn't here.'

'And why's he not here?'

'Because I'm still here.'

'And when's he coming?'

'I don't know.'

'So how are you going to find each other?'

'I'm not looking for him.'

'Why not?'

'When two people look for each other, they miss each other. I'm waiting for him.'

'How will he recognize you?'

'I'll do the recognizing.'

'How?'

'I'll know when he comes.'

I stopped speaking, cleaned my glasses. My father shut the pot of glue. His glasses were white with dust too. Such an important person, Death, and my father wouldn't recognize him in the street, not even if he was standing right in front of him.

'And he's definitely coming?'

'Yes.'

'Mine too?'

'Yes.'

'Then I'm waiting now too.'

'It can take a while though,' my father said.

'Then I'll get bored maybe.'

'That's very possible.'

I lay down, like I'd seen people do in films. Always, when Death came visiting, people were lying in their beds, sleeping, and it was very quiet. I pretended to sleep. I pretended to be as pale as the woman downstairs and lay with my arms crossed for half an hour.

My father was hammering the legs of the chair, hard, into the seat. Death was never going to come with all this racket.

'It's boring. Do you not get bored waiting?'

'No.'

'Why not?'

'I've something to do.'

He put the chair back down and my mother opened the door.

'What are you two up to?'

'We're talking about life,' he said.

TAT WAS SITTING LIKE A KING on his new chair, stroking the armrest and explaining that not all REASONS and ARGUMENTS belong in the Encyclopaedia of Good Reasons, even if they're unbeatable.

'The Peroxide Blonde's cousin's got nice hands.'

'That's true. And he's really very good with them.'

'He was a master thief, the best in the town where he used to live.'

Tat looked at me.

'Who told you a story like that?'

'Toni. He also says he had to come back from Abroad because Abroad doesn't want him any more cos of his success.'

'Did he say whether he's still working?'

'He said he's on Incapacity, in Switzerland especially, cos of the many dangers lurking here. He says it upsets him, not being able to work.'

'I understand.'

'Why does it upset him?'

'It's exhausting to have to forget your trade if your tools are part of you.'

'Why?'

'There's too much heart and soul involved.'

'What page of the encyclopaedia will we put that on?'

'We're not writing anything. First, we'll think.'

I APOLOGIZED QUIETLY.

'Louder,' Imelda's mother said.

'Finally,' Eli said. 'When's she getting out?'

'Any time now. We're driving.'

She was the Flower of the Month. Imelda was laughing again, a ray of sunshine again, and 'my girl' in the eyes of her father, who kissed her and lifted her out of bed although she'd been able to walk again for ages. He carried her in his hands to the poster with her picture on it, in the hospital corridor. She was an example to everyone as regards how quickly you can get better again, even if nearly all your hair has fallen out cos it no longer trusts your head.

My parents and I were waiting with flowers in the corridor. Imelda's father put her down on her feet, wanted to see her walk. He wanted to see her walk every day, and today especially. Imelda was getting to go home. To be the best again. The cleverest. Her profession, it was.

The first thing we did was take Imelda to the hairdresser's.

Hair was the absolute domain of Madame Jelisaweta. There's no one better, Mirela says. She'd already had every type of hair in her hands, even did Imelda's father's bald head well. She didn't always cut completely straight. And it was known for people to have to slant their heads for a week cos Madame Jelisaweta didn't like correcting what she'd done. She'd the kind of perfume, though, to which you just surrendered—nothing else mattered any more. She also wore huge ear-rings that waggled, had a smile that included gold teeth and a face my mother called a wilderness cos Madame Jelisaweta's eyes were the colour of the green hell of the jungle.

Madame Jelisaweta shook her head. Imelda's hair was thin—the scar, glowing through it. She put her scissors away and gave Imelda a gift—a hat.

'*Voilá*! To get you started.'

She looked over to me. She wanted to go for a short walk, a short talk. The rings were waggling in her ears and clinking, she bent down and smiled in a way that made me dizzy, and whispered in my ear, 'That will get you nowhere, sweetie. With a shovel, wasn't it? That will never get you anywhere. Do we two understand each other?'

I nodded. You had to have lost your mind to pick a fight with Madame Jelisaweta. It was as foolish a thing to do as baring your arse at Oskar after tormenting him for an hour.

But what was I supposed to do to make them stop? To make them stop *that*? To stop them talking, stop them sniggering, to make them finally give me peace, to stop them whispering, stop them shouting out windows, stop them chasing me, chanting: *Orphanage brat*!

With Imelda leading the way.

Orphanage brat.

The fattest encyclopaedia beside my bed didn't have that in it. The feeling was all I had.

'So that was that,' Tat said, the following Sunday.

He stopped stroking the armrest.

THE TEACHER WROTE THE ESSAY topics up on the board.

'"A Seaside Holiday" and "Mother and Father". You can choose. Anyone who has never been to the seaside can write about mothers and fathers. Everyone has those, after all.'

Blank pages cause problems.

Eli took it lightly.

'Make something up.'

Full pages cause problems too.

'Hard to believe, what's written there,' the teacher said.

'Hard to believe,' my parents said. 'Who's she talking about?'

They wondered if what I'd imagined could become real again. The doctor would have to check. The essay, I had to rewrite. From scratch, the teacher said. *As a matter of principle. In principle*, an easy thing for you to do, he said. He gave me the essay back.

'What's *principle*?'

'Primarily, *principles* are *laws*. That you keep to. I want to see the essay tomorrow.'

'I can't write about it, I've never been to the seaside either.'

'By tomorrow.'

MY PARENTS HADN'T A CLUE about the seaside. Unlike Imelda, who had gone there with her parents for the *experience*. She could've written two pages about it, no sweat, she'd said, and a novel about her parents. Eli would've known what the seaside is but he'd gone to a building site that not even my father knew. Other than that, only Long-Distance Werner could know.

I rang the Peroxide Blonde's doorbell, with my essay in my hand. She'd a thick paste in her hair, took the essay from me, rolled it up and killed a fly with it.

'Fleabags! You needing sugar?'

'No. Where's Long-Distance Werner?'

'In Saudi Arabia. Why?'

'When's he back?'

'In a week, if everything goes to plan.'

'That's too late.'

'What for?'

'The seaside.'

'The seaside?'

'Do you know the seaside?'

'Certainly do. Want nothing to do with it. The sea scares me. Always did. What's more, it ruins your hair,' she said. 'Salt and sun—pure poison!'

She pointed at her head.

'Time to wash that out.'

'Can I have it back?'

'What?'

'The essay.'

I put it back in my jacket pocket.

Madame Jelisaweta was my last hope.

Her salon wasn't especially big. The day Imelda was given the hat as a present, it was bursting at the seams. It wasn't an official hairdressing salon and certainly didn't belong to Madame Jelisaweta but to our landlord, for whom she'd so many lovely-sounding swear words, Eli occasionally asked her to curse for him when something he called *Swiss bureaucracy* had left him speechless again. Madame Jelisaweta wasn't always open either. The salon, alone, wasn't enough to keep her head above water, so sometimes she lent a hand elsewhere. I was in luck though.

On the walls were pictures—Yugoslavian seaside town, Yugoslavian forest waterfall, Yugoslavian river landscape in an international sunset, Yugoslavian world-famous gorge and Yugoslavian pop star, or fading star in the Yugoslavian pop scene, depending on who was looking. The pictures were curling at the corners, the climate in Madame Jelisaweta's salon being a problem for them.

She was just filling little bottles and let me sweep up hair for her. Madame Jelisaweta was very particular about that—she wanted to be able see what she'd done all day. Once she'd straightened up all the hair lacquer containers and scrubbed the combs and brushes clean in the wash hand basin, she put coffee on.

'What have you done wrong this time?'

'Nothing.'

Madame Jelisaweta screwed up her eyes. With her cigarette in the corner of her mouth, she opened a jar of olives. She always kept a few inside her cheek, to spice up conversations.

'And what's that there?'

My essay must've fallen out of the bag. She lifted it.

'An essay.'

'And you're coming with it to me? What does it say in it then?'

'Nothing special.'

'Show me.'

She read, whistling through her teeth, clicking her tongue. Read on. Spat the stone from an olive into her hand. Her cat brushed against her legs.

'I have to write a new one.'

'And you're surprised?'

Not even Madame Jelisaweta appreciated the essay about my parents, though she was used to a thing or two—swearing in at least five languages, all kinds of shapes of heads, all kinds of hair colours, switching to a new brand of cigarette, a family that had scattered all over the place, astronomical phone bills and the economic miracle that had created more work than she could ever have allowed herself to dream.

'Do you know the seaside?'

'Yes.'

'Can you tell me about it?'

She lit a second cigarette and put it down on the ashtray.

'Which one do you mean? There are various ones. Even just in Yugoslavia. Even right outside our door. The seaside with sun or no sun. Wind or no wind. In stormy weather. The seaside from a ship, the water or when you go diving.'

Her cigarette burnt away in the ashtray as she told me about grass under the water, about hedgehogs that don't like milk, and stars at the bottom of the sea that her brother brought ashore—where they immediately lost their colour. On days off, he jumps from the cliffs, and they fry fish on the beach that's made of rock, burning hot stone where salt glistens, and in the night that follows, there's a storm, a *swell*, with waves as big as houses that can wash a meadow away, just like that, along with a tractor, a dog and a goat. They'd almost swept her brother away too, who had gone out with Uncle Jernej. He'd made it back in the broken boat just in time, didn't know which way up he was. On board, it had been raining fish, he said, Madame Jelisaweta told me, dead fish and living fish.

My ears were buzzing.

'And your Uncle Jernej?'

'He never came back. He's a fish now. A lot of fish.'

She threw the olive stones in her hand away.

'What's the time saying?'

From the window, you could see the clock on the church tower if you leant out. In Madame Jelisaweta's shop, that wasn't especially dangerous. If you stood at the window properly, you could see beneath women's skirts. That was also a reason why Madame Jelisaweta's salon was a tip for those in the know for men, and an absolute must for ladies. I screwed my eyes up.

'Just before two.'

'Then you'll have to go. I have a customer in a minute. I'll write down the title and the first sentence for you.'

'A Seaside Holiday.'

You first see it with your nose . . .

'Your turn now.'

AT HOME, I MADE A SEASIDE BOX, and the first words to go in were *swell*, *rough sea*, *heavy sea* and *sea urchin*, *sea weed*, *starfish*. I filled the bath, tipped two kilos of salts in, blue bubble bath, I blew up my swimming ring and got into the water in my clothes. A storm came along. And what a storm. A wind, at the very least, like when there's a foehn storm at the Walensee. The waves as grey as powdered stone, big and getting bigger. Walls, actually, dark walls, black. Waves with no idea where to go next. Furious, they set upon the ship. Waves higher than Madame Jelisaweta described, bigger than she could imagine. Waves as big as houses, as tall as towers, as high as mountains. Crashing waves that send everything spinning, that foam and roar, that pull the sky down into the water, that salt the clouds, move heaven and hell, that turn your head and shake words, shake and shake them till they break—*crashing waves* splinter, are now *washing craves* and *carving washes*, *craws heavings* and *caves wingrash*, are flotsam now, everything's flotsam, everything's being tossed round—the sky, the water, the boat. It's raining crates and dead fish from the cargo area.

My mother pulled me out by the hair. At that moment, I was Madame's brother, who had fallen overboard, screaming and spluttering, and managed to grab the life belt at the last minute. The sharks had come up close already. Dangerously so. Bad sharks. Hungry sharks.

'Half the bathroom was under water,' my mother said at the kitchen table.

'Have you written your essay?'

I shook my head, just. My father looked tired.

'Scram.'

I HANDED IN THREE PAGES. 'A Seaside Holiday'. The teacher was impressed, even if I'd strayed from the theme, as he put it. *Far* too many people had died in the three pages for his liking. The town that had still existed on page one had been washed away. And, in the end, just a starfish had survived. He found that particularly sad. He looked at me for a while, then let me go.

IN ITALY, TONI'S SISTERS WERE SO WORRIED that they were losing weight, just about—though Switzerland had such a good reputation. It was for their sake Toni had gone back a bit earlier than planned, leaving only a jar of olives behind. Now my mother was so worried that she was losing weight. For three weeks now, she'd been harping on and on to my father about Italy. He was sick to the back teeth of her hellish misery.

She wanted to see the sea.

She wanted to have mozzarella.

She wanted an experience.

She didn't want to end up like Tatta who'd had to be given pills by the shrink for the dullness in her heart, for atrophy and darkness.

'What's *atrophy*?'

On the table lay Toni's letter and a wooden box Aunt Joujou had sent. It was a bit bashed but otherwise in one piece. The postman had been trying not to touch it as he handed it over. It stank terribly. When Eli arrived, my father took the lid off. Inside bulged a furry cheese that looked like it would explode any minute.

'From Joujou. From France.'

Eli nodded appreciatively and my mother took him over to the windowsill where the photos enclosed with Toni's letter were now displayed. A picture of his sisters, one of the fields of tomatoes, one of his parents' house, of his parents, of the mental asylum, of the church, the market, one of mountains of watermelons, one of mozzarella on a plate. Eli wiped his fingers, then studied it closely.

'He takes photos of cheese?'

'He has an artistic vein.'

'She'd like to go to the seaside.'

My father knew the seaside only from other people's stories. That you can just sit there, watching the water come and go, that you can simply drift along, on the beach and in the sun, were things he hoped to confirm. He looked at Eli, as if to ask. Eli shook his head.

'But it's coming into fashion.'

'We've no money for fashion.'

My father stuck the spoon in the cheese and pulled it back out, gently. He could make the longest cheese strings. If he'd taken it into his head, he could've been the world-champion cheese-string maker.

'What's wrong with you at all?'

My mother snapping at Eli was nothing unusual. Her also throwing a cloth at him was. Even my father would now think harder about fashion.

But Eli just lifted the cloth, took his cap and left.

You couldn't do much with him, of late. That was cos of FOREIGN INFILTRATION. Toni had only just been passed by the REFERENDUM. He'd be allowed to stay here, for now, when he got back from Italy. His plastic moulds were a winner in the factory, and what he did many another night was known to no one but the galvanizing plant and it was keeping mum. Madame Jelisaweta wasn't a problem for Switzerland any more either. Only Eli couldn't be sure. Dejan and Mirela had promised to hide him in the cellar of the restaurant with the cheese and beer if things got risky.

Eli could sense FOREIGN INFILTRATION with every fibre of his body. The REFERENDUM hadn't meant that the ISSUE had gone away, his pals said. The immigration police were on Eli's tail, they said, as part of an attempt to remove some FOREIGN INFILTRATION and send it back where it came from. The police, more and more often, were turning building sites upside down, wanting to see permits. That made Eli very nervous.

I walked behind him, confident he'd go to Snow White's hutch, the only sensible place, apart from the toilet, where you can think your thoughts without being disturbed. I caught up with him when he sat down.

'What are you thinking about?'

'I'm not thinking about anything.'

'So what are you doing?'

'I'm waiting.'

'What for?'

'Nothing to happen.'

'You can't wait for that.'

'I can. Wait for nothing to happen that would make things even worse. You can certainly do that. Have to, even. Hijos de puta! Sons of bitches!'

If you're not stronger than the people you're calling HIJOS DE PUTA, you shouldn't even think of saying it. Eli used it only as an exception, for the concierge, for the immigration police and for a Mr Franco who was known to everyone in Spain. Not even Eli would say it out loud though. It was in the word box labelled TOP SECRET, along with at least another hundred names for concierges and the immigration police in Spain, Italy and Yugoslavia.

He sat down and kicked the case of rabbit food. Two screws and the nameplate for his room were in his hand. The incredibly long name filled three lines. The bucket with his tools he put down beside Snow White's feedbag.

'I can't go back.'

'To the building site?'

'To Salamanca. To Spain. To anywhere.'

'Do you have to?'

'The police want me to. I'm a seasonal worker.'

'What's a *seasonal worker*?'

'You know, sure. Like Toni. A seasonal worker can work here for nine months.'

'But you work all the time here.'

'That's true, I'm also twenty per cent illicit. What's more, I *was* a seasonal worker.'

'What does *illicit* mean?'

'That the quota has been filled.'

'And what does *quota* mean?'

'It means I'm now one hundred per cent illicit.'

'And what does that mean?'

'Means I've no papers. Nothing. Nada. Coño! Shit!'

'Why have you none?'

'I've the wrong ones. They're Spanish.'

'I've the wrong ones too. I'll only get the right ones once the adoption's complete.'

'It's not so easy in my case.'

'You need to get yourself placed.'

'Who with?'

'Parents.'

'I've got parents.'

'And what?'

'They're dead.'

'We could share my artificial ones. You're a welcome guest here, till death almost, my father says.'

Eli sighed. He polished the nameplate with a corner of his pullover and took a screwdriver out of his pocket.

'Why did you unscrew it?'

'I need to be careful.'

'You could take on another name. Once my adoption's complete, I'll have a new name. We need to be careful too. Cos of the original parents. They could get stupid ideas and get all sentimental suddenly, Ruth and Walter say. Are you living down beside Dejan's cheese and beer now?'

As he didn't answer, I tried to encourage him, said it could've been worse, that is, a cellar full of vegetables, of fennel, or celery or even more disgusting vegetables. He'd hit it lucky with a cellar full of cheese and beer. What's more, once a month, he'd have the company of a suckling pig—as he knew, first-hand, himself. Dejan insisted on fresh produce that had still been running round as he got ready to make his suckling pig and sausages.

He'd stood up, now opened Snow White's door and screwed the nameplate inside it. Snow White scampered round, in the cage.

'Tell your father my post should come here now.'

'Is there police in Spain too?'

'Of course.'

'Like here?'

'Worse. Much worse. But it's not quite as bad these days.'

'Were they after you there too?'

'They were after my family.'

'What happened if they caught someone?'

He pulled a face as if the doctor had just given him a big fat jag. He looked as if he was chewing something.

'Why'd you come here?'

'I heard here was better, easier. It wasn't easy at home. There, nothing was.'

On each of his fingernails—a white moon. He spread his fingers.

In the bucket were a trowel, screwdrivers and a board with a handle, sponges, the board he called a rubbing board, the rubber beaker in which he stirred a paste that he used to fill holes in our house, and a thick ruler that a bright yellow bubble moved to and fro in.

'Is that all you have?'

'It's enough to build houses.'

I threw a handful of stones at the fence. Oskar growled.

'Stop tormenting him.'

'What did the police want your family for?'

'Is it possible to know?'

'You don't know?'

'My sister. They wanted my sister. One just came and took her.'

'Why?'

'He liked her soul. *He* said. Soul—don't make me laugh! Cabrón!'

'You can't just get a soul, my father says. Unless you sell your own to the devil.'

Oskar started pawing the ground at the fence. Eli scratched his back with the trowel. He looked like he was thinking.

'She never came back. They took a lot of people in Salamanca. There's hardly a home without someone missing.'

'So many?'

'Yes.'

'Everyone?'

'No, some always escape.'

'Abroad?'

'Or to Heaven. Heaven's full of angels.'

The priest had said God says the soul goes straight to Heaven. Whether it can also do a detour, via abroad, he hadn't mentioned.

'Why did you prefer to go abroad?'

'For a clever girl, you ask some pretty stupid questions.'

Maybe the priest hadn't listened to God properly or God had mumbled. I'd have to phone Tat and ask. He was closer to God than the priest already, he *knew* things, though he'd tell you otherwise. Tat liked it when I asked him prickly questions. It tickled him, he'd giggle as he looked for an answer, would need time to find one. His head has many rooms.

'Not all the rooms are still lived in. The childhood one, definitely not. I have to go down into the cellar for that,' he said.

Tat needs more than fifteen minutes to go down to the cellar and back again.

BIRD IS ON HIS TRAVELS TOO. Towards evening, he flew off. Bird likes to go into the grass and trusts cats. What will become of him?

My father can't console me.

It's sure to come, sleep, el sueño. I'm waiting.

Where's Bird?

I put on all the clothes I have and leave the window open. My mother comes to close it—asks why I'm heating the garden.

Bird's not from here, he likes it warm.

Heaven's full of angels.

I can't heat Heaven.

FROM HIS HOLIDAYS, TONI BROUGHT US BACK a lot of Italian and not much German, large jars of boiled-down tomatoes, a huge piece of crumbly cheese, mozzarella that was swimming in water, two cans of olive oil and three of wine. Even *thinking* about all the carting he'd done, he broke out in a sweat again. He was wearing black. His mother had died. He didn't want to talk about it.

'It was expected.'

When he heard Bird was gone, he raised an eyebrow, and when he heard my mother had had fifteen funerals in his absence, I got a clip round the ear. I'd have liked to tell him that Eli now had to hide from the immigration police but my mother told him first. Toni dug his toes into the carpet. And when I told him Eli was spending whole days down in Dejan and Mirela's cellar and then at Snow White's hutch, that Snow White was now called Snow White de Eliseo Álvaro Manuel Raúl Caballero Pardo and had been keeping Eli's post for him since the day he'd screwed his nameplate to the inside of the hutch, I got another clip round the ear. Toni turned as pale as the mozzarella he was slicing at that very moment. He put the knife down.

'Are they looking for him?'

'Of course.'

'In the building too?'

'They were here once but not even we knew where he was at the time.'

'Do you know now?'

My mother shrugged.

'This place one minute, another the next. Why all the questions?'

I couldn't keep my mouth shut. I was the one, after all, who fed Snow White, not my mother. I was the one, after all, who met Eli when he collected his post or put something in the shed. I was the one, after all, who had brought him matches and a packet of spaghetti from the cupboard so he wasn't tempted to eat Snow White. I was longing to say something, as my mother seemed to be able to tell.

'Not another word, understood? You haven't a clue what you're talking about. And you don't know where Eli is, where he's staying. We don't either, and definitely not if anyone asks. You know absolutely nothing, if anyone asks. Once and for all—nothing! Is that clear? Or you'll end up getting us in hellish trouble. Out!'

'It's all right. Leave her alone.'

My mother was in a state Tat called the overwrought-nerves-phase. Whenever she was in the overwrought-nerves-phase, you could only nod or shake your head, depending. Even Tat then considered it better to keep his mouth shut or to pretend he was deaf, he'd put a smile on as if she'd just brought him a cup of warm milk and honey. Tat could do that because of his advanced age when it's hopeless, anyway, to try and train someone. I wasn't allowed to, though. I nodded.

Her handbag fell on the floor. Amazing, how much there was space for in there. She swept it all into a pile and stuffed it back in.

'Is Eli at your place?'

'I've just said, we don't know where he's hiding.'

She raised her eyebrows as she spoke and kept her eyes firmly on Toni and me.

'Are the police coming back?'

'How should I know? What is it about you? Why are you asking all these things?'

'Are we going to walk a bit? Let's go out, come on.'

My mother didn't answer. They both said nothing for a while. They just looked at each other. Looked at me from time to time. Looked away. Anywhere. Finally, Toni smiled, the kind of smile the Peroxide Blonde would have to eat three of her favourite pink cakes to produce.

US NOT SITTING ROUND TONI'S FLAT any more suited my father too. He was of the opinion that my mother could do with some fresh air. When you visited Tat, you could see what happened when he just sat around in the house cos the weather was so bad. His face wrinkled even faster than his apples in the cellar. It seemed, of late, as if he'd taken them on in a race—and no way did my father want my mother entering the wrinkliness race too, if the garden was already *his* job alone, and was keeping only *his* complexion as fresh as that of the vegetables.

My mother and I would meet Toni at the door. Over a period of weeks, they kept inventing more new words for the walks. I wrote them all down. The teacher was glad to correct them. He was pleased and called them *expressions* each time I turned up with a new one. What my mother had, he said, was quite a bit of *inspiration*:

They went out *for a little dander*. (Short, just.)

They went *for a breath of fresh air*. (Round the corner, only.)

They *stretched their legs a little*. (To get out for once.)

They went *for a walk*. (After all, the sun's shining.)

They went *for a stroll*. (Despite the rain.)

They *wandered along* in the wind. (That bit of wind won't hurt.)

Toni got a head cold and couldn't get rid of it.

It got to the point where they went for an *amble*. The supreme discipline, my mother called that. It helped you relax, as did sitting in the pastry shop afterwards. They must've been very tired. They would let their coffee go cold. There were long pauses. It wasn't because of Toni's German. And my mother's German was in perfect working order. She was also used to helping others with language for hours on end, if they were stuck for a word in their own. Now she herself had none, and when she and Toni did speak, they took me by the hand.

If the teacher asked was there a new *expression*, I'd to shake my head. My mother's *inspiration* had possibly run out. She started misplacing things—shopping lists, keys, her most expensive lipstick, money. She even forgot her film afternoon at the Peroxide Blonde's place—the TV premiere of a film about the African savannah—just the two of them, champagne included.

To take my mother's mind off things, I smashed a window on the main shopping street. Smashing windows was one of the worst things you could do. Aunt Joujou and her could spend all day talking about the windows that were smashed in Zurich. Even if that was two years ago now, those windows were legendary. Even Tat was flustered. He wanted precise details. Had the insurance been hit too? he asked, repeatedly.

My mother's jaw dropped, then stayed that way for days. She couldn't explain it to herself, my father was at his wit's end too. On Ruth and Walter's advice, he stopped my pocket money completely. They were seriously worried about me by phone.

I was worried about my mother. I decided to show her the EXPRESSIONS word box so she wouldn't be tempted to forget me somewhere again. Maybe it would also help her and Toni in their search for words, and be an inspiration. I was really excited when my mother—amazed—read: EXPRESSIONS. She stroked the wood.

'One of Tat's cigar boxes?'

I nodded. As she read, my mother changed colour almost as quickly as the squid that had been on TV last week. She looked at me as if a ghost had crossed the room behind me (white), threw the box at the wall (red), and the EXPRESSIONS fluttered in all directions. Any other time, she'd always liked what the teacher liked. Only in this case did she seem to have completely different taste. Without a word, she left the room, slamming the door behind her. The EXPRESSIONS rustled, and FOR A BREATH OF FRESH AIR landed at my feet.

I remained seated, came close to calling the fire brigade. Tat had drummed it into me, in an absolute emergency only to call the fire brigade, not the ambulance, cos the fire brigade's faster, no matter what. In this country, a house is more precious than a human being. Tat was convinced of it.

I phoned Tat, but it was only the neighbour who answered, and she wanted to talk about the plum pie that was in the oven at that very moment, and about the tree the plums came from—a tree that was making Tat anxious because it was making another neighbour anxious as it was as old as Tat and rotten, hadn't yielded much fruit for years now. She then mentioned the garden that was looking forward to my father coming because Tat just sits around and waits until the fruit's ripe now, and he could sleep through even that sometimes, despite the many alarm clocks and clocks in the house.

I whispered into the receiver that Tat was a very important man in the fire brigade and was needed now like no one else on earth. She took a deep breath and snarled at me, said, none of you lot are right in the head, and hung up.

My suitcase was under the bed. I pulled it out, stared at it. I'd arrived here with it. I sat down beside it, opened it. I smelt it. It hardly smelt at all. I took off my glasses, it smelt stronger. I tried to lie down in it, but it was too small. No matter how hard I tried, no matter how much I curled up, I could find no more space in it, and so remained seated beside it. In my head, I went through the Encyclopaedia of Good Reasons from front to back, twice. I found nothing that helped. Not in the fattest encyclopaedia either. With encyclopaedias, you always need to already know what you're looking up.

When my mother came back, she gathered up all the slips of paper. There was the scent of fresh lemons in her hair. She handed me the box and asked me to step on it.

It was already dark when my father came into the room and asked was I planning a journey, and if so, to let him know. I'll go with you, he said, regardless of where, today had been hell.

'Why you sitting in the dark?'

He turned the light on.

'You seen Eli?'

I shook my head.

'We're about to eat. So? How was your day?'

Since the conversation with Ruth and Walter, he'd been wanting to see some successes. Fact was: EXPRESSIONS had definitely not been a success, at least not in my mother's eyes. EXPRESSIONS didn't help either, when it came to INSPIRATION that had run out. If my father found out about those things, I could take my case and go and join Eli. And wait. Like Eli. Wait for nothing to happen that would make things even worse.

'No, I haven't seen Eli.'

'That's OK. Come and eat now. Did you not hear us?'

WITH ONE EAR FIRMLY ON THE PILLOW, I'm lying in bed.

No light flashing, none flickering. Later, a light that wanders. The baker drives off, his car buzzes. He hasn't far to go. The car's new, a beautiful red. He likes to take it for a run. Rain—swooshing, drumming, on the tins of hardy words out on the window ledge. The room is green, due to the night-light in the socket. Sleep is refusing to come.

Eli knows this feeling too. But he's full of pictures. I'm full of nothing. The green doesn't help against the blackness that's worst at night.

It's sure to come, sleep, el sueño. I'm waiting.

THE WORD BOXES GOT ON MY MOTHER'S NERVES cos they were getting bigger and bigger, were bursting at the seams and sometimes toppling over, were on the bed when she wanted to change it, blocked the desk I was to do my homework at, and the view. They piled up on the windowsill too.

I got on my mother's nerves cos I wanted to have the boxes everywhere with me. Wanted to cart them with me to Tat's. To Aunt Joujou's at the Walensee. It also got on her nerves that I could never decide which to take and so ruined things for everyone else as the food would be cold cos we'd arrived late—because of me. And I'd then be miffed all day (as my mother put it) as I'd lifted the wrong ones cos I'd been rushing—because of her.

Her last remaining nerve snapped—my doing again—when I took word boxes down into the cellar, where bags and more boxes with screws and nails in them stood around, and my father, cursing, took some up to the kitchen as all these word boxes meant there was no more space in the cellar, and my mother was cursing too when she found screws in the cutlery drawer, and slips of paper with borrowed words written on them, or a German word or an emotion. Emotions don't belong in the cutlery drawer, screws and nails don't either. Cutlery drawers full of emotion are an *absurdity*, and if my father didn't want to sleep on the sofa again, he'd better not insist in her presence that it was more a *challenge* for the brain or an *interesting assumption* or a *mental exercise.*

CUTLERY DRAWER, my mother wrote on a slip of paper before sticking it on the drawer. CHINA CABI-NET, she stuck on one door, having found tacks, nuts and plugs in it, as well as my GATES box. She was just correcting the spelling to GAITS with a thick felt tip when the Peroxide Blonde turned up and put her favourite pink cakes—piled high with cream—down on the table and asked had my mother lost her mind, had her memory broken down or what, if she was having to label the kitchen to know where things were.

My mother pulled a drawer open and took out a handful of fork-word-nuts. She plucked out a few slips of paper and read them aloud to us: 'MISERY, WOE, SOR-ROW, GLOOM—all in with the forks. TO BE IN THE DOLDRUMS and all. And in with the spoons? What have we here, besides screws? PASTIME, BOREDOM—'

She turned to the Peroxide Blonde and put every-thing down on the table.

'And you're telling me not to lose my mind? Look at that. No one would believe it otherwise. Oh, what am I saying? There's no point.'

TO THE CUPBOARD, SHE SAID, 'What kind of place is it I'm living in? I could just as well go away to the circus. I'm going away to the circus. It would be easier to control a crowd of monkeys. Three lions? A piece of cake. I could teach a herd of elephants to walk in the garden without crushing as much as a primrose. After three weeks, they'd been dancing the tango in pairs in the kitchen and not even an egg cup would get smashed.'

She got so worked up, the Peroxide Blonde just nodded, slurped her coffee, sucked the pink cherry on the top of every cake, let spoonful after spoonful of cream melt in her cup before seriously tilting the cup for the last swig and, saying cheerio, going. My mother didn't even notice. I gathered the slips of paper, careful not to get in her way. My mother was capable of anything. She could throw words in the bin, she could, and I'd have to fish them out again.

'Where do you find them all?' Eli had asked.

'Tat saves them for me. My father rattles off words as he drives. My mother has words galore, my father says. And then there's school.'

Eli admired my parents. He couldn't find a lot of words, even in Spanish. He'd simply no time to look for them. Every house he started building had to be finished soon.

My mother locked a lot of words away. She'd only ever given me a single word box, right after Ruth and Walter's first ever visit, and we were lying on the sofa and she'd decided certainly not to invite those two to her funeral. She'd yet to stop writing things down and reading them out. The words came in a specific order, couldn't be in any other order. I couldn't remember them. They meant nothing to me.

'Use an *aide-memoire*.'

My mother—half-French, of course—swore by *aide-memoires*. Hers always worked. Mine didn't aid you at all.

'And yet, she said, it's really easy. I'm your mother—if all goes well, that is. I have a sister, she'll be your Aunt Joujou. Her two sons will be your cousins.'

'I don't like them.'

'That doesn't matter.'

'It does.'

'Not at this moment, it doesn't. Tat will be your grandfather. His three sisters and four brothers, your great-uncles and great-aunts.'

'But I don't know any of them.'

'That doesn't matter in the least! Just listen. Tat has parents, they'll be your great-grandparents, their brothers your great-great-uncles, your great-great-aunts—they're all dead, your great-great-grandparents too, of course. Their children are first cousins of Tat's uncle who'll be a great-uncle of yours, and his one son is our first cousin. Or, to be more exact, he *was*, he died in a car crash. His children, in turn, will be your second cousins, and the great-grandchildren of Tat's father's brother will be your third cousins.'

'Do I know them?'

'No. And then you've brothers and sisters.'

'I don't.'

'Let's assume you've a brother.'

'What does he look like?'

'How am I supposed to know?'

'Have I one after all?'

'Not that I know of.'

'Or a sister?'

'There's nothing about that in your records.'

'Did you check properly?'

'Let's just assume you've a brother, I can then explain it to you.'

'What do I need all that for?'

'What do you mean *all that*? It's *family* we're talking about.'

THIS WAS AN EMERGENCY, like burnt-down olive trees, the Walensee in a foehn storm, Ruth and Walter up in arms, or my mother's hellish misery that could strike as suddenly as winter at Tat's place in the mountains. The kind of emergency that had me close to phoning the fire brigade. I thought I'd try Toni first. I'd to ring five times before he opened. He shifted from one foot to the other and blew his nose. His nose was really red.

'It's been running. For weeks. Just refuses to get better.'

'Can I come in?'

'Not possible.'

'How come? It's urgent.'

'Let's go for a walk.'

'I don't want to go for a walk. I don't want a runny nose too. It's really urgent. I'll have to call the fire brigade otherwise.'

I held the jotter out to him. He blew his nose again and sighed.

'If you like. But you can't stay long.'

In the kitchen, he poured me a glass of milk. I pushed it away.

'You need to read it.'

He opened the jotter, flicked through it. They'd spread it out over eight pages, one word per page. YOUR FATHER WAS A NOBODY, YOUR MOTHER PAPER.

'Who wrote that?'

I shrugged, and Toni downed the glass of milk in one.

'And what am I supposed to do with it?'

'What am *I* supposed to?'

'Tear the pages out.'

'Then they'd be missing.'

'So what?'

He raised my chin and looked at me.

'You *do* have parents.'

'I do.'

'But?—Sit down.'

I'd told Imelda my parents had ordered me from a company whose job it was to make sure we found takers on time. It had sold me on a commission basis. My mother had seen me as a golden opportunity but Imelda said her mother said I'd never be the real deal, as a daughter. It's like the price on a plate, Imelda assured me, really hard to remove, and something always sticks to it later.

'You were the one they picked. *You*.'

I didn't say anything.

'What?'

'I'm not exactly the jackpot.'

'Says who?'

'Everyone.'

Toni tilted his head.

'And what else are you? A shining star, maybe? Exactly, a shining star.'

'A brown dwarf.'

He took me in his arms and tried to comfort me. Toni obviously hadn't a clue about the sky at night. Or brown dwarfs were called something else in Italy.

'And you've still some growing to do.'

The buttons on his shirt blurred, my nose was running, I was wetting his shirt. We remained sitting, I don't know how long. He gave me his hankie. Tat was the only other person to have such big ones.

'And put your glasses on.'

'Can we play hide-and-seek?'

'No, it's not possible.'

'Why not?'

It was the same as ever, after all, I was the same as ever, I wasn't even that much bigger, everything was the same as ever, everything was as before, before the holidays. Toni smelt of lemon, the room of a small coffee, the sofa was prickly, you could hear the water pipes, the carpet was giving off fluff, the clock was ticking, the TV downstairs was blaring, his pink newspaper was lying on the table. It even got on my mother's nerves—all this having to hang around outside all the time, having to put up with his head cold, the sniffing and sneezing, the red nose that made him look a bit less like a film star, on Sundays too. She thought it was idiotic. He got up and turned the radio on.

'Wait here. You're not to budge an inch. I'm going to get cake and then you have to go. Promise?'

I nodded. He was already in the hall when he came back to call in.

'Chocolate cake?—And you're not to budge an inch, OK?'

Without waiting for an answer, he banged the door shut.

In Toni's bedroom, it was dark. I opened the curtains. Before, we used to play hide-and-seek, under the bed included. Now, he didn't want to any more. He refused, saying I'd got too big. Since his holidays in Italy, I was too big for most things—and for a lot of others, still too small. I wasn't allowed to wear his things any more, to run through the flat in his shoes, to flutter across the room in his shirts playing Bird, to fill his dead uncle's leather briefcase with paper and selected pink newspapers, to write lists and measure him with the measuring tape—that is, play the authorities and legal guardian—yes, playing Ruth and Walter had been childish since after his holidays. Jumping on his bed, forbidden—pillow fights ruined the bed-linen though he used to laugh, before, when a pillow burst, though three of us, at the same time, had even jumped on his bed till the slats popped out. He'd had to put them back in, cursing as he did. Half a boxful of Italian had come out of him, by which I don't mean my smallest word box either.

The bed, the alarm clock, the chair with three legs. The fourth one lay beside it. Like before his holidays. Under the bed, the boxes full of photos and plastic flowers in a bag. The magazines, the rolled-up carpet, even the ball was still there. The air had got out of it. What's more, I still fit under the bed—I'd have to show him.

The old chest, the carpet with the pale colours, the chest of drawers, with one badly scratched. In one drawer, an old clock and books, clothes in another. They smelt good. Of lemon. Just like everything smelt of lemon, even the pictures of saints. Beside the chest of drawers, in a box, lay screws, a hammer, pens. Still more clothes. Some my size too. He seemed to have brought them back from his holidays, like the big new wardrobe. I opened it. Inside the wardrobe sat a girl.

I shut it again and took my glasses off. You can't believe your eyes when they're glazed. I reopened the wardrobe.

The girl was still there. I touched her.

She squeaked.

I smelt her. She did indeed smell.

Good.

Of raisins.

I put my glasses on again.

'What are you doing in there?'

She didn't answer. Just sat there on a crochet blanket, gawping, in silence.

'Are you playing hide-and-seek? Toni's gone out. You can come out.'

She still said nothing when I opened the doors wide. The inside of the wardrobe was covered with photos. I sat down on the floor in front of her and pointed at the biggest photo.

'Who's that?'

I'd to ask twice more.

'Come on. Who is it?'

'My mother.'

'Who?'

She spoke as quietly as the Peroxide Blonde when rummaging in her mailbox for post.

'My mother.'

'You mean artificial too?'

'What does artificial mean?'

I could hardly understand what she was saying. She looked at the floor as if she might find words there.

'Does someone bring you words?'

'What?'

'You could do with some, that's for sure. Were you expensive?'

'Children don't cost anything.'

'What do you know! Where's your mother?'

'In Heaven.'

Heaven—she stretched the word a bit. This and every other word, she stretched at the wrong end. It was as if she pulled at them, and at some point they seemed to get caught on something and snap back. The rest she just swallowed. She'd a big gap between her teeth and all. I'd have liked one too. Natural Disaster had been able to spit nearly three metres through his.

'Are you from abroad?'

She shook her head fiercely.

'So where are you from then?'

'From home.'

She wasn't very big, and pale as cheese. A lot of hair. Long. Curls like my mother would've liked me to have. Eyes like my most beautiful marbles.

'Can you stay here?'

'Don't know.'

'It's the same everywhere. Do you never come out?'

'In the evening. And sometimes if my father fetches me.'

'And who's your father?'

'Toni, of course.'

'So you are from abroad after all. That means you're a foreign infiltration too. Like Eli.'

'What's a foreign infiltration?'

'Something they don't know where to put.'

She stared at her bare feet. Her toes were digging into the crochet blanket. She pulled the doors slowly shut, asked me to go, to say nothing, to nobody, ever.

I remained in front of the wardrobe for a while.

'I'll bring you words. You need words.'

I put my ear to the wardrobe door.

'Everyone needs words.'

Nothing stirred.

'Do you need sun? I can bring you one.'

Still silence. Even when I closed the curtains, nothing stirred. I put everything back where it belonged. I did what I did when I searched my mother's bedroom for hidden sweets.

SNOW WHITE WAS AS SILENT AS A GRAVE. So silent, she even gobbled up Eli's post so no one could find it. Eli's pals had been packing it in a lunchbox since and Snow White would sit on it and enjoy the better view.

Dandelion and lettuce, lettuce and dandelion—you could thrill Snow White with that, she'd gobble it up as quickly as the electric vegetable-shredder in the kitchen at Dejan and Mirela's restaurant.

You could have a real conversation with this rabbit. Snow White understood, would pull the dandelion in through the wire, and I could let everything out—say that I was getting sick to the back teeth, gradually, of foreign infiltration. That I was sick of the sight of it. That it hadn't even existed in the Home. The Housemother had always kept a spare bed for emergencies. Even for emergencies like Natural Disaster, a bed had always been free. I explained to Snow White that the Housemother just had to make sure we found takers on time and didn't go mouldy in the Home, that the quota was met, and that we, if possible, should shift like warm rolls, the faster the better. That it was known she'd come to us from the fruit-and-veg trade and hadn't lost her preference for fresh produce. That was why she was a cleanliness fanatic, an ironing-creases engineer, a sandman-removal specialist, a Swiss-trained fingernail-checker, an ear-examiner and sock-inspector. It was also known that nothing could irritate her more than peach or grass stains on clean clothes. Not even Natural Disaster would've dared to sit on a peach deliberately or slide round on a meadow. We had to be fresh. As fresh as lettuce. Or dandelion.

Viewed like that, it wasn't going to be easy to find a taker for Eli. Fresh was something he really wasn't any more. The white moons he had under his nails, from plaster and paint, would've had the Housemother in a complete and utter rage.

I paused for a bit. Snow White was chewing and grinding the food. I had her full attention:

'That said, there would've been no question of foreign infiltration for the Housemother, cos of what her job was. There are no secret compartments for human beings. *Clothes* belong in a wardrobe. Nothing else.'

I kicked against the bucket with Eli's trowels. Snow White stopped eating.

'You heard right. In the wardrobe,' I whispered, 'she's really living in the wardrobe. She has to remain a secret. Toni's hiding her there. Most of the time, she says.

He's hiding her from us. In that kind of wardrobe, there's less space than in your hutch. Comparatively less.'

I swore to Snow White, on the dandelion in all the meadows, that I'd check every single cupboard to see whether any more foreign infiltration was trapped there, maybe even Eli. You never know. I opened the lunchbox. It was empty, no post for Eli, nothing. It occurred to me I'd forgotten to ask the girl her name.

'I don't even know what she's called.'

Snow White blinked, I buried my head in her fur, asked her rabbit-tummy, 'What will we do now?—Where on earth is Eli, and where is Bird?'

BIRD, TONI SAYS, IS SURE TO HAVE FLOWN up into Heaven. Such a long journey, he says, but don't worry—he'll find the south all right.

The teacher says he's an *atheist*. He doesn't believe in Heaven as a place of residence. My mother's also an *atheist*, she says. She's relieved there's a name for what she has. Heaven isn't possible in her eyes. She just can't get a hold of it.

'But one thing's for sure,' the teacher says. 'There's no south in Heaven.'

How can you visit someone who doesn't exist, I asked Tat the following Sunday.

'In your head,' he said.

He asked me to fetch the picture of Tatta from the windowsill and wiped it clean with the sleeve of his cardigan. I only knew her from stories. All of Grisons had fond memories of Tatta and loathed the shrinks who had put her to bed with a pickaxe and shovel. They said shrinks were rich-people-stuff, that rich people are a class, a different class that lives almost exclusively in the lowlands, only strays into the mountains to take the waters, and then their eyes glaze over when they see the beauty of it. Once up there, they also get a red face and woolly ideas from the fresh air and the sun they underestimate, just as they do every storm and the snow that—only on postcards—doesn't ruin nice shoes.

'The Parterre Swiss!'

'What do the likes of them know about us?'

'Nothing.'

'And what good was Tatta's shrink? She's dead anyhow.'

'Poor soul.'

'May God rest her soul.'

'No one could cook potatoes like her. Do you remember her *maluns*?'

'Gorgeous.'

'And her polenta?'

'Unforgettable.'

'Her *Gämspfeffer*, even more so.'

The whole of Grisons remembered her cooking. It was world famous there.

EVERYTHING THAT TAT HELD in his hands trembled. Cups, plates, fork, the clocks he wound up, the fruit he'd hand you, Tatta in the picture. She trembled, especially. Tat could hardly hold her—little Tatta, broad Tatta. In her worn-out shoes and with a bunch of flowers in her hands, she was standing at a fountain.

'But she's dead.'

'So what? She often visits me, and I visit her.'

'Where?'

'Here. And in places I went with her. It's really easy. You can do it too.'

'No, I can't.'

He wanted to know why I was neglecting the Encyclopaedia of Good Reasons.

'Because.'

'There you go! Yet again. You need to find better reasons than that. *Arguments*, as I say. Haven't I told you before? Also, visiting her's really easy. It always works. Phone me if you were with her, won't you?'

With one ear firmly on the pillow, I'm lying in bed. My father's snoring, my mother's snoring, the neighbour curses, the door into the garden opens, Oskar farts—they've given him the ends of the garlic sausage again from Dejan's restaurant, so he has to sleep outside now. He turns and turns on his own axis on the piece of cardboard under the porch, I turn and turn, he's whimpering in his sleep already, I turn and he's dreaming he's running, I can hear his paws pawing, I can hear everyone sleeping.

It's sure to come, my sleep, mi sueño. I'm waiting. When I wait, nothing happens.

'SHE'S CALLED MILENA,' I told Snow White. 'Toni calls her Mili.'

I pushed dandelion through the wire, carrot peel and the left-over lettuce my mother had given me for her.

'Mili likes popcorn and the colour green. She thinks her hair's boring. She says it's normal in Italy, where she's from, she'd rather have blond hair. In her opinion, mine is much more boring, even darker than hers, half her relatives have hair like that. What's more, Switzerland's to blame for her having to sit in the wardrobe, she says, and Toni says. Also that those immigration police guys are just *pencil-pushing farts* and never make any progress. She says their brains are like fridges. Her grandmother's life had been too short for pencil-pushing immigration-police farts, she didn't have the patience for it, had given up, her grandmother died and that's why she couldn't stay in Italy, and Toni can't go back to Italy cos things are going so well for him with the little plastic moulds and there's the galvanizing plant too. Finally, he can begin to imagine having an olive grove in Italy again. *Pencil-pushing farts* is her favourite word and green her favourite colour—her absolute favourite.'

I wrote *pencil-pushing farts* in chalk on the stone slabs.

'We have to remain secret, she says, she mustn't ruin it, she says, Toni says the olive grove now depends on her and that he's doing all he can to make the wardrobe as nice as possible for her.'

'Are you making any progress out there? It's about to start raining. Clean it out, I said. The hutch has to be shining.'

From the window she'd just cleaned, my mother was keeping a close eye on me. I bent down to Snow White and rolled my eyes.

'Ruth and Walter are coming.'

To be on the safe side, I wiped *pencil-pushing farts* off the slabs.

A *DISASTER* WAS WHAT RUTH AND WALTER'S VISIT WAS, a complete *disaster*. A *disaster* was something there are no words for. After it, my mother just wanted to find a taker, by which she meant someone who hadn't lost their senses.

Foaming with rage beneath the tree with the nicest view, she unpacked her sandwiches and tore the plastic hood from her head. It was drizzling.

'Who do they think they are?'

Without a word, she ate a whole sandwich. She seemed to have forgotten me.

Ruth and Walter had got on the wrong side of her. Why I didn't know. She wasn't telling me, it wasn't suitable for children. She went on to arrange a funeral that wasn't suitable for children either—Ruth and Walter's. It would be neither poignant nor beautiful. She assured the cemetery it could start bracing itself, if ever those two were sent to Hell.

No one would want to see a funeral like it. Especially not in this weather. It was coming down in buckets. The few cars that had made their way here got stuck outside somewhere and sank in the mud. The funeral party, a few official faces, had to wade its way through the puddles and streams. The priest was bedridden and sent a replacement who didn't know the way and so arrived late. The coffins had started to rock in the water that had gathered round the graves—Walter was soon listing heavily. Eli and the groundsman had decided to fill the graves in again as quickly as possible. Because of the rain, the brass band had been cancelled anyway, apart from two trumpets, and when the priest's replacement finally arrived, with wet shoes and soaking notes, Eli was smoothing the soil over and had to put up with being asked which of the two was now in which grave.

'And Eli being Eli, he hasn't bothered with anything like that. The rain deals with the rest. Sweeps even the wooden crosses away. Pulled out of the bushes by the river, they are, days later. You couldn't imagine rain like it. The fresh graves all emptied, the grill of the weir flecked with floating flowers and the official wreaths. And, at the cemetery, no trace of the pair of them. Not a thing. As if they'd been a bad dream, just. After only a week. Time is a great healer.'

'POPPYCOCK!'

Time isn't a great healer. Tat had so many wounds to complain about, he ran out of breath trying to list them on the Sunday and had to lie down. He ended up having a coughing fit and in a bad mood.

'Who's talking such nonsense? My daughter-in-law? As for the dead being thrown away after twenty-five years, did she invent that too? They stay where they are. For all eternity. Full stop! They just get more company. That's all.'

The description of the funeral impressed him though. He sat up in bed and asked me to straighten his legs, one had fallen over.

'So?'

'What?'

'Have you visited her?'

'Who?'

'Tatta, of course. Didn't I ask you to.'

'I can't do it.'

'Do it the way I said. In your head. Bring me the picture.'

Tat stroked the frame.

'Wasn't she beautiful?'

I nodded. Tears were running down his face. Tat was in an odd mood.

'The woman next door's beautiful too. She takes care of me. Occasionally, she bakes me a cake. Nothing's working right any more.'

He pointed at his legs and held out his saucer to me, the cup on it was trembling, and when he tried to pour himself some coffee, he spilt some. I'd to bring him a cloth and really had to stop myself from saying there are others worse off than him, that others have lost the grandmothers they depend on and are now trapped in Swiss wardrobes, and that getting to them was complicated cos they weren't allowed out, cos they didn't exist, unlike Tat who was sitting in bed like a king, whose pillow I puffed up for him any time he wanted, and my mother brought him milk and honey, and apples from the cellar, a cellar full of apples my father had picked for him. Tat, who could move around, if only he wanted to. If he'd strap his legs on, he could go out into the garden, still enjoy the garden a bit before the snow fell, snow he'd been feeling in his bones for a week and had been able to smell early this morning.

Tat turned to the wall.

'Don't forget to put food out for Sepp. And tell your father to wind up the clocks. All of them.'

WITH ONE EAR FIRMLY ON THE PILLOW, I'm lying in bed. I'm not allowed the light on. And I'm not allowed to read in poor light. It isn't good for my eyes. They're not the best as it is. I'm not allowed to strain them.

Reading too much isn't healthy. It has consequences. My mother can think of enough examples.

Uncle Theo, a queer customer.

Aunt Tilde, an old maid.

The woman downstairs, dead.

Readers, my mother says, never get married, have children's hands and talk to themselves in their old age. If they have an accident at home, no one notices. Books can't call an ambulance, they don't shout into the receiver, don't interrupt what they were saying, don't cry or fetch help. When someone's forced out of their home, they play along. Without a murmur. Box after box of them from the cellar was taken away to Vienna.

It's sure to come, sleep, el sueño. I'm waiting. On an opportunity.

'CANCER ATE MILENA'S GRANDMOTHER ALIVE, I told Snow White. Who'd have thought a star sign could do that.'

Snow White nibbled at the carrot I'd brought her.

'Milena says she's memorizing the heavens, the stars and all, so she'll find her way round OK if ever she has to go there. It can happen very quickly. As quickly as in the case of the mother she can't remember, or the case of the grandmother she misses a lot. She says Toni says she got ill after he came to Switzerland to work and that it was to be expected she'd die. Everyone was just hoping the grandmother would be able to hold out till Toni had sorted out everything in Switzerland. But Switzerland can't sort things out that quickly cos Mili's an international matter. Switzerland reckons his daughter should go to her uncle in Germany or stay in Italy with one of the sisters. But Mili can't possibly stay with one of Toni's sisters cos she can't stand any of the four, and Germany's already got enough on its hands with Toni's brother and reckons Switzerland should look after him as Toni, after all, is working here and Mili is *his* daughter and not his brother's. And now she's here. But it's not the end of the world, Toni says, he tries to console her and he's doing all he can to make the wardrobe comfortable and beautiful. There's even a light in it and wallpaper on the insides. And a mirror! We looked at ourselves, together, in it, and I told her Tat's secret: Blink, blink once, and if you're lucky, the image will remain in your head for ever.'

When Snow White was done with the carrot, I pushed in a load of dandelion. Dandelion, clover and plantain—her favourite meal. Incredible how much crap Snow White could make from fresh green stuff. Ever since I'd fired rabbit droppings at Imelda at school, everyone wanted some. I picked them out of the darkest corner of the hutch, wrapped them up in bags and swapped them for comics and chewing gum.

In Eli's lunchbox was a letter from the police.

'FROM THE POLICE?'

Tat raised his eyebrows. I nodded.

'Does your father know?'

I shook my head. Tat rubbed his chin. It sounded as if my father was sanding wood. Tat stroked the armrest of his favourite chair and pulled his cardigan tight.

'Did you open it?'

Again, I shook my head.

'Is it still there?'

'Don't know.'

'Is Eli coming to get it?'

'Don't know.'

'Where is he?'

'We don't know.'

'What's he done then?'

'He got nabbed. Day before yesterday.'

'Doing what?'

'Working.'

Tat pursed his lips and reached for a Toscani. Nothing else could fall off now, his legs were already away. He puffed at his cigar with his eyes closed, sighed, then asked, 'He didn't get away with a black eye?'

'He got one of them too. But the guy he'd hit the evening before had a broken nose and reported him to the police.'

'He was in a fight?'

'Just a bit of one, his pals from the building site say. They'd to go for witness questioning, my father says. And it came out that Eli's not even allowed to be here. What's *witness questioning*?'

'The police ask you something and you absolutely have to tell the truth. It's better to, anyhow. In most cases, anyhow.'

Flies were circling in the thick Toscani cloud. One landed on Tat's nose. He waved his hands to get rid of it. A bit of burning ash fell on his cardie and burnt a hole in it.

'Mierda de giat! Lumpamenta!—Scumbags!'

Next thing, he was just looking at me. For a long time.

'Will I tell you something? I saw Tatta today. Very clearly. And if you want to know the details, she was sitting right where you are now. Not a cheep out of her. That was all she wanted—I asked her. Did you see her too? Outside, maybe?'

I shook my head. He was quiet for a while and stubbed his Toscani out in the saucer.

'I'm tired. I'd like to be alone now. Leave me alone.'

In the old spin dryer in the garden, Tat grew the best strawberries. My father was piling wood in the wash-house. Tat seemed to collect wood. I learnt—*plywood*, *slats*, *strips of wood*, *veneer*. PLANKS I knew already, my father piled them on shelves. He rolled half the tree trunk from one corner to the other, then hammered the axe in and left it there. Next, he sawed bits off that would fit in Tat's stove and I put them in baskets.

'Tat can see Tatta.'

'What?'

He put his saw down and took the cotton wool out of his ears.

'Tat can see Tatta. She sat down beside him.'

'Is he in pain?'

'He didn't mention anything.'

'And what's he doing now?'

'He wants to be alone.'

'Let him sleep. I'm nearly finished. Put some more wood in the kitchen. The good stuff, from Curdin.'

'There's a letter from the police in Eli's lunchbox.'

My father leant against the wall, looked at the dust swirling round the light bulb, then flicked the switch on the saw again. It got going with a screech. He put the cotton wool back in his ears.

At home, I put PLYWOOD, SLATS, STRIPS OF WOOD, VENEER and PLANKS into KINDS OF WOOD. My father had made me a box at Tat's and carved KINDS OF WOOD on the lid. I ran my finger across it. The lid smelt bitter.

'Nut,' my father said. 'Walnut.'

'I BIT MY TONGUE TWELVE TIMES, fifteen times, I didn't tell anyone anything, not even Tat, and I've put aside three biscuits, two chewing gums and half a cup of toffees,' I told Snow White. 'I've put a Batman comic in under your straw, and spent all my pocket money on popcorn, to share with Milena. Now I've no money to pay Imelda off—she spotted me pocketing the Batman. I'll have to throw her in the river. And I can't count on you either, I see. You've gone and eaten Batman.'

I held the tattered pages out to Snow White.

'Where's the rest? Without the rest, you can't read it. What's the point of me bringing you all the green stuff?—and Toni wants to speak to me. I don't want to speak to him. Switzerland needs to make progress for Milena's sake—and my father says we can kiss the adoption goodbye, if they catch Eli at our place. Cos they'd then pin an *illegality* on my father. Ruth and Walter would disapprove of that more than dust and rotten oranges. My father says the authorities will say parents like that are a bad example and wouldn't be able to care for a child from inside a prison.'

I kicked against the fence till Oskar started jumping at it and baring his teeth.

'If the Mili story comes out, the adoption will go down the drain. My parents will be fetched by Uncle Eugen like Natural Disaster's father, I'll have to go back to the Housemother and will have a mountain of records cos of all this for sure, and Milena will have to go to one of Toni's sisters till Switzerland has sorted out with Italy when Toni will have to go back to Italy cos he has an *illegality* on his plate too. And Tat will have to go into a mental home cos he can see Tatta. My mother says that's nearly as good as seeing pigs fly. She says she doesn't want the adoption going down the drain cos of my father, who has a lot on his hands with Tat already, and now he has foreigners round his neck too. My father's in trouble with her again cos of the foreigners. Cos of Eli, above all. He's volunteering to sleep on the sofa.'

'Do you think Tat can see flying pigs too?'

'SEPP IS DEAD.'

He was an old dog, true, but it wasn't old age he died of.

'Full of lead,' Tat sobbed into the phone. 'His body's full of lead.'

He asked us to come. Now. Right away. The woman next door was at her daughter's on holiday, so couldn't bury Sepp. Tat couldn't bury Sepp either. Not with his legs, he couldn't. The hunter had simply left Sepp at the door with a slip of paper with the words *Two deer*! on it.

I tried to comfort Tat by telling him Sepp was now with Tatta, and Tat said:

'Put my son on.'

Tat too could really struggle sometimes with the Encyclopaedia of Good Reasons.

My mother refused—just because of Sepp—to drive to Tat's midweek. Something was to become of my brain. So I had to go to school.

'Tell him we'll be there in three days, anyway. And when are you going to see to the tap?'

My father, twisting the flex in his hands, asked Tat was it still freezing hard during the day outside, then asked him to put Sepp in a box behind the house till Sunday. Behind Tat's house was quiet, especially in winter when the snow grew round the house, slid down off the roof, swooshed down out of the trees that, at night, snored and grumbled like Oskar in his sleep. You could even hear the snowdrops falling—however much they tried to be quiet. The sun never shone there, the snow stayed there the longest. Tat had told us he'd been able to walk straight up onto the roof to check the chimney, back in the days when he still had both legs, all his teeth and an eye for the women all right. My father sighed and opened a beer for himself.

'The tap's dripping.'

'Just a little.'

'But it's dripping.'

'I know.'

Dripping taps were a thorn in my mother's flesh. They left scale marks. And although Sepp had just died, they were leaving some now.

'It won't stop dripping all by itself.'

'I know.'

'I kept telling Tat to put Sepp on a lead. He'd more fleas than hair, and he was an old dog already—how old actually?'

'Twelve.'

'And how's Tat?'

'He's crying.'

'He'll recover though.'

'He has always recovered.'

'Put a lot of food out for Snow White on Friday.'

My father was pacing up and down in front of me. My mother took a hellish misery pill.

'And water. Snow White needs enough water.'

'Where do I put it in?'

'Help her with it. I'm off to the shops now.'

Through the crack of the door, she shouted:

'And fix the tap.'

Forty-two drips. That's how long we were silent. Then my father went to get his toolbox.

'From now on, we can only visit Sepp in our heads,' I told my class. They were impressed that Grisons would deep-freeze him till we got there.

FOR THE WHOLE JOURNEY TO TAT'S, my father was kneading the wheel.

'Sepp is in good hands.'

He nodded in the driving mirror, the nodding dog on the back shelf nodded back, and my mother smoked a cigarette. Rain was spraying in the window. I closed my eyes, in your head it wasn't far—where to?

'She's as white as chalk. Pull up.'

My mother had turned to me. He stopped in the bend with the pine trees where I fell out of the car, practically, and stomped round in the snow till my stomach was no longer turning, the road was no longer swaying, the door was still and the cold air was no longer nipping me. My father thought the cold air was great, he held some snow against the back of my neck, shook the frost down from the young trees and got back in, glistening. He drove more slowly now. He was crawling. It had started snowing.

Tat, wrapped in a blanket, was tottering up and down outside the house.

'Stupid dog,' he said. 'I'm sure he bit the hunter and all. Blood was running from his ears.'

Tears were running from Tat's eyes. He held out his thumb, beaten black and blue by the hammer as he nailed Sepp into the crate.

'He's in a crate? We can just leave him there then.'

'No way! I want to see him again.'

Tat wiped his eyes. My father had his hands in his pockets and was stamping the snow down.

'Brass monkey weather, this. Where is he?'

'Behind the house.'

'Doggone weather.'

'There's really going to be snow now.'

Tat held his nose up to the air and seemed satisfied. The sky he was looking up into was brushing against the gable. Further back, it was swallowing the trees. I was catching snowflakes, the roof would soon have snowy candyfloss on it, and icicles—we'd be able to build a snow-Sepp. My mother said:

'Great, a white funeral. Go and get your coat.'

My father needed a crowbar to open the crate and he lifted Sepp out. When Tat looked at him, as if to tell him off, he tapped the ground with his pickaxe.

'Brick-hard already. You digging or am I?'

Sepp was lying in the snow, his fur dotted with small holes. In the middle of his forehead was a big one. He looked like he was sleeping, was no doubt hunting deer in Heaven, leaving fleas on the clouds like he did on the carpet, fleas that bit as much as he did. It would soon be raining fleas, snowing dog hair, his fur would fall from the sky, the brown hairs, beige hairs, black hairs, the soft, the gentle hairs, the hard, bristly hairs. Doggone weather! Eli's pals, up on the shell of a building, would curse.

The snow made caps for the trees, the bushes, made pearls for my father's hair, then a cap, a cap on top of Tat's cap, and a blanket for the vegetable patch as they stood beside Sepp, and Tat went on and on at my father, with puffs of steam coming from his mouth, until my father went away, fetched the pickaxe and started to hack at the ground as if it was its fault.

Tat had asked us to stay the night. He wasn't at ease. Tatta was pushing him, he claimed, was standing in the garden and giving him hell, he was finally to get himself over there. The Jordan, as the river was called, wasn't as deep and wasn't as cold as you thought. Tat was afraid of the water, though, and a coward into the bargain. Tat didn't want to. It would be much better, he said, if Tatta would see to the burglars—yes, burglars—who were getting up to mischief in the garden, hanging around the front of the house, just waiting for the opportunity to clean him out like a Christmas goose, any which way.

'When was that?'

My father looked at him, puzzled.

'Here? Your place? And what was stolen?'

When my father asked had he informed the insurance, my mother said oh-great and Tat moaned about the insurance and his legs for half an hour and went red in the face, but what had been stolen, he couldn't say, even after all that. He'd forgotten. My father went through the important things—the documents, the little box with Tatta's jewellery, the sugar bowl with the money in the kitchen, the motorbike in the garage, the tools, they were rusting and covered in spiderweb, and my father shrugged his shoulders but Tat stuck to his story and said:

'They'll be back, you'll see.'

My parents looked at each other. We took Tat to bed. Growling, he lay down. He wanted to make a paper boat.

'Bring me some paper.'

He nodded, smacked his lips and reached for my hand.

'And now my milk and honey. Get me some milk and honey.'

In the kitchen, my mother, shaking her head, pointed at a pan crawling with animals and mould. She flicked through the unopened letters. There was even one from the insurance. My father sat down beside Tat's bed.

'Why don't you read the post?'

He put down the half-finished boat.

'You see, they took my glasses too. Even my glasses—imagine. Grascha putana, how are you supposed to cross the Jordan and see what you are doing?'

The glasses I found the following day in his trousers where he must've put them instead of in his wallet. They were in pieces, with him sitting on them. It had nipped his behind all right but at his age, he said, something else hurts every day. You mustn't take it seriously or you'll go mad.

'What do you think of my boat?'

We stayed longer than one night. My father was piling wood for days, carrying it from here to there cos the *there* was closer to the house than the *here*. Tat was complaining, he had his stick in his hand, was poking at the snow with it—the *there* wasn't OK with him either, wasn't easy to reach, not with legs like these, they weren't, not in weather like this, not without the woman next door, not without Sepp who was able to fetch help if it all went wrong and he fell—the snow, of course, would silence any cry for help.

BENEATH THE SNOW, IN THE OLD SPIN DRYER, Tat's best strawberries were sleeping. My father had pulled on two pullovers and one of Tat's cardigans and was sitting in the garden. It was completely quiet. It was late and he was starting to put things away, was looking in the snow for tools that Tat had taken into the garden but not put back. My mother wasn't saying much either, wasn't even complaining about the stink, the dirty shirts hanging on nails in the wall, the buttons that had come off that Tat collected on a plate, the cardigans with holes in them.

Tired, she killed the last of the wasps that had survived inside, and wound up a few clocks on the walls. Tat hadn't asked her to do anything more.

'Tat's losing it,' my father said as he baked an apple in the stove.

Two nights before, he'd nearly killed him with his shovel when the light of a torch was darting round the garden, when someone really *was* moving round the garden, and he'd discovered it was *Tat*, who cursed and said he'd be pressing charges against the swines who had stolen his time. They'd stolen it out from under him, he claimed, in broad daylight, and now, presumably, they wanted to kill him, what else would they want? He asked my father to help him catch them. My father couldn't tell whether he meant the days or the thieves or Tatta, who Tat roared at not to stand around doing nothing on the bank of her stupid river, and he only managed to calm down when my father promised him an apple, braised in the oven, a soft, sweet apple, one of those stored in the cellar that had wrinkles and were crying out to be braised and eaten, and I wanted one like that too, they were the best apples there are. You couldn't get them anywhere else. My father found fault with all kinds of apples, just not with these, nothing, not at all, though they'd lots of wrinkles. They smelt of honey and of Tat when he'd shaved—and it was a different apple-smell from Ruth's—he smelt softer, sweeter, not as fresh, maybe of the cellar where the apples all lay, a cellar-and-apple-smell that made its way further and further through the house and got into the clothes cos Tat was always forgetting to close the door, or didn't have the strength to any more, a smell that faded from the clothes when Tat had worn them for too long and that appeared again when the shirts and trousers were washed or were hanging on hooks, aired, like now when Tat was sitting beside me before the open stove while my father made his bed again and my mother closed the door to the cellar, we sucked at the apples from a bowl, he burnt his lips, cried and gave me a riddle to solve, much trickier than any I'd ever thought he'd know. He said, 'I want to go home.'

MY FATHER DRUMMED HIS FINGERS on the kitchen table, stood up and put on more wood. He went out to the front, where the beech firewood was piled up to right under the roof, he trudged through the garden, testing the snowdrifts that led up to the house, looked up to the sky, listened to the night.

'Snow will be up to the windowsill soon.'

'We'll take him with us, in that case.'

My mother went into the cellar to pack some apples. My father crumbled whatever he found on the table—a bit of this, a bit of that. What it had been wasn't clear any more—all kinds of animals had fled to Tat's kitchen before the snow, eaten him out of house and home nearly and left behind a fair amount of dirt. My mother'd had a bout of hellish misery as soon as she smelt the kitchen.

'Christmas soon.'

'In a week.'

'Help me pack.'

'Am on my way.'

I skipped through the kitchen like Muhammad Ali, ducking round him and throwing my best right punch which he blocked with a grin.

'Get a move on.'

I gathered up Tat's legs and the unread letters, the woollen cardigans with the big holes so my mother could darn them. I threw what was left of the polenta into the yard where I could hear the hiss of the cats. My father then threw the pan out too, and two broken plates, a cup full of rusty screws and nails, some light bulbs, a few broken tools, mountains of apple cores, tiles full of Toscani butts, Sepp's collar, a woollen blanket that moths were living in. The thing was, Tat had clean ones, new ones. My father found them, still shrink-wrapped—gifts from my mother. He then went round with a shovel and a brush.

I sweep the yard, shovel the snow and blanket up into the bin. Also—snow with moths, plates with snow and moths, bits of broken plate, cigar crumbs, animal-wool, woolly-animal-nails, apple-core-screws and spanner-snow, light-bulb-rust and snow-polenta. My mother breezes out of the cellar, cellar-apples in her arms, an apple-cellar smell in her clothes. They put the mattress out into the night. It's a mattress-night, a bed-linen sky, the stars are falling, nearly, the snow glitters and shines, Tat's sitting in his armchair by the stove, he opens the door of the stove, pokes round in the embers, spits into them, causing a hiss, and—in a really bad mood—chews at his collar.

'Soon be Christmas, Tat.'

'Not even a lousy week, Whippersnapper.'

'You don't have to eat your collar. There are cookies for Christmas.'

'I'll let you into a secret. Do you know that during the war we'd to eat a dog?'

'A Sepp?'

'No, a mongrel with black and white spots, a curly tail and poison in its veins—pure poison, not a drop of blood. Otto. I swear to you, Otto didn't stand for any nonsense.'

Tat grinned and scratched the stump of his leg.

'Tatta had patches at the ready. For the backsides of all the postmen's trousers Otto tore to bits.'

He sniggered.

'They even dared to keep delivering bills during the war. And us with nothing to eat too!'

'You're in great form again! What kind of horror stories are you telling her now?'

My father had come in so quietly we didn't hear him.

He rattled a box of nails at Tat's face, the biggest nails I'd ever seen.

'You need these?'

'At least we'd ration coupons. And Tatta's foresight. Three days before rationing was introduced, you once told us, she bought polenta. A whole kitchen-cupboardful.'

'Yes, weren't there only eleven of you?'

'That's right, and you ate all the sausage yourself. Every time.'

'It wouldn't have been enough for twelve anyhow.'

'Thirteen. Counting Tatta. So—do you still need these or not?'

He pointed at the box in his hand. Tat dismissed him with a wave and poked me in the chest.

'Anyway, Whippersnapper, we had to eat Otto.'

'You really all ate Otto?'

'*He* wanted us to eat Otto.'

'That's enough, you! Now let me finish the story.'

'You'll be giving her bad dreams.'

'But I want to hear it!'

'You want to hear every cock-and-bull story.'

Tat was a bit offended, almost. He stretched in his chair and arranged his legs.

'It did happen, after all.'

'Bad enough in itself.'

My father turned and slammed the door shut, making my mother curious enough to come in.

'Everything OK?'

'Just perfect! Can you get me a coffee?'

'So what happened to Otto?'

'We didn't eat him.'

'No?'

'No, there were a lot of things wrong with Otto but he'd really gone too far that time. No idea what got into him. He went for the butcher's child. Bad, it was. The boy'd to go to hospital. The doctor didn't want to go near his arm. Bad, it was. Very bad.'

'And then?'

'Then the butcher wanted me to shoot Otto but I couldn't do it. So I took Otto along to him, thinking, we can kill two birds with one stone here. There wasn't much meat back then.'

My mother put Tat's coffee beside him. Tat nodded and waited till she'd left the room again. He tipped some coffee into the saucer, splashing it all over his trousers and cardigan.

'And then? Keep Going!'

'Then the butcher brought me a joint and two legs. Strips of tender meat.'

'Just for the heck of it?'

'Course not. It was Otto he was bringing. Miarda! Otto, cut up into portions. Otto, served up professionally by the butcher. Tatta put too much salt in, with her tears. He smelt good, Otto, and the better he smelt, the more of us started to bawl at the table, and your father cried the loudest. Tatta refused to take the joint out of the oven and when the thing, burnt black, was finally in front of us, your father puked in his plate, as true as I'm sitting here. But I wanted them to eat him. He'd been served up to us, after all.'

'And then?'

'Tatta wanted me to start.'

'So?'

'I threw Otto out of the window. Into the garden.'

'And then?'

'No "and then". We didn't eat that day. Didn't eat at all that day. It was a Tuesday, I can still remember. How long your father was angry with me, I don't know any more. I think it's continued to this day.'

There was a shrill buzz, from three clocks on the walls, chains rattled and, one after the other, three cuckoos shot out and cuckooed. The fir cones on the chains were swinging. I'd have loved to have a cuckoo. But Tat wasn't for parting with one. They seemed to be an important part of the clock, like the bubble in Eli's spirit level. Tat looked out of the window for a while, massaging his stump.

'It's the right. Always the right.'

'What?'

'It's the right foot that hurts. Burns, it does. Like fire.'

'The plastic one?'

'No, the other one, of course.'

'The one that no longer exists?'

'What other one could it be, Whippersnapper?'

Tat slurped the cold coffee from his saucer. Rubbed what he'd spilt into his cardigan.

'We're going to have more snow.'

'I don't want to eat Snow White. And not Oskar, either.'

'Who's Oskar?'

'You know already.'

'Do I?'

'Our neighbour's dog. There's a lot wrong with Oskar too.'

'Like what?'

'His farts are horrendously loud and he pees against everyone's legs.'

Tat laughed so much his teeth fell out. I'd to lift them up and rinse them, and before I gave them back, I made him swear not to say anything, not even by accident, not to anyone, ever, he'd to be as tight-lipped as Snow White when it came to what I was about to tell him.

Tat was all ears.

'TAT KNOWS,' I TOLD SNOW WHITE. 'Tat knows everything. He even knows that, to begin with, Mili wasn't even allowed to go to the toilet when Toni was at work cos you could hear it flushing right through the building. To begin with, she had to use the potty. Till she got used to being a secret. One that's a ticking bomb, she says, says Toni. One that has to be quiet, to crawl round, that isn't allowed to laugh, to shout and certainly not scream, isn't allowed to put the light on and, if need be, has to eat in the dark. Tat was really impressed by that. He said it's like during the war. And that those immigration police ones are pencil-pushing farts is something he's known for longer than I've been alive, he says. He's known it since the war. In his opinion, they can do more harm than any insurance company, and that's saying something if it's Tat that's saying it—Do you know how long it will take me to separate these? And it's all wet here—look.'

A mixture of droppings and grain lay all over the hutch. I'd put in a fair amount of food for Snow White. And my father had arranged a tube for Snow White to suck water from. He didn't want to risk anyone going near Eli's post, even if a rabbit was guarding it.

'Tat knows too that Mili's grandmother was eaten alive by something. He doesn't think it was her star sign though. Cancer, he says, is an illness. And he wants to know where Eli is. There are whispers in the stairwell, I tell him. Do you know, Snow White?'

WE CELEBRATED CHRISTMAS with traditional sweet biscuits. Eight different kinds.

Brunsli—chocolate, with almonds.

Mailänderli—lemon-flavoured.

Chräbeli—with aniseed.

Zimtsterne—star-shaped, with cinnamon.

And another four that didn't turn out right.

My mother was at the end of her tether, my father exhausted. Tat had been here for a week and not slept a wink. He slept badly in strange places. He missed his clocks and had to go outside to smoke his Toscani. At night, he wandered round the flat in his dressing gown and haunted the stairwell. My parents hadn't slept a wink either, they were constantly having to go and fetch him. Once, he was in Toni's flat and took off his legs and refused to leave. Toni carried him down, put him down on the sofa, then handed my mother his legs. Tat sat beaming at us. Then he seemed to wake up and looked at Toni and me before taking out his dentures to see if his teeth were still all there. He'd done that every day since he arrived.

'You never know. In town, everything vanishes before you've had a chance to look round, hardly.'

My mother could only relax at the Peroxide Blonde's place. She'd sit on the sofa, be served little pink cakes, dip them in her coffee and sigh. She didn't need to say anything. The Peroxide Blonde had met Tat a week ago. He'd rung the doorbell, got her out of bed at five in the morning and held an empty cigar box out to her. For quarter of an hour, he'd tried to explain what he needed. With his teeth out.

THE TABLE WAS SET, extended for the big crowd. Aunt Joujou had, personally, brought fresh baguettes, half a carful of French cheese and wine, stale bread in a bag for Snow White and, for me, a yellow raincoat, strong enough to take the Walensee, or any sea you care to think of, it smelt like a blow-up mattress. The Peroxide Blonde decorated the plates with pine twigs and even before the meal, Long-Distance Werner had phoned three times to speak to her from a town he couldn't pronounce the name of. Each time, by the time the Peroxide Blonde finally got to the phone, he'd been cut off again. I was under the table, admiring Henry and Silvester's huge shoes.

My father had threatened single-handedly to throw Father Christmas and Aunt Joujou out onto the street, and her baguettes after her. He swore too that he'd use Joujou's cheese to blow up the French embassy in Berne and give all her wine to the drunks at the train station if Henry and Silvester weren't invited too.

Those two were impressed by Tat. In Africa, it's a huge deal if someone makes it to old age, actually manages to live that long, they explained. To mark the occasion, Tat had his suit and both legs on. Henry and Silvester wanted to see them. True wonders of technology. As engineers, they knew that to see. There was no comparison with what you could get back home though legs were needed there more often than here—there was always a war happening and war had it in for legs. Tat was proud of his Swiss legs, of the joints manufactured in Sulz. He explained the technology, cursed the insurance company only briefly, showed them his new glasses too and listened to what Henry and Silvester had to say about the fire-sauce they'd brought from Africa in jars. A sauce that refreshes Africa and makes Europe's ears ring. So hot and spicy, the chicken would fly out of the oven any minute now, they said. Tat nodded and folded his napkin into a boat that he put in his soup bowl. While we waited for the chicken, he tugged at the sail till he got it right and kneaded the hull. A trickle of spit was running from the corner of his mouth.

'Where's Eli? I want to see Eli.'

'Eli can't come.'

'He's missing at the table.'

My father gave him a long look and Tat made his boat all over again.

'Give me your plate.'

'It smells delicious, looks it too. I experienced the war as a guard on the Austrian border. That and rationing. We even ate the dog once. Where's Oskar? I want to see him.'

He was poking his fork at my father's arm.

'Stop that, will you. Oskar's in the garden.'

'Come on, I want to see him. Now.'

'Tomorrow. We can go down tomorrow. The chicken's getting cold.'

'I want to see him now.'

My mother took a hellish misery pill and suggested going back to the tree with the nicest view tomorrow. Back to Almost-No-Feathers too, anything, to get out of this madhouse. There was no calming Tat. We'd to help him up and over to the window where my father whistled for Oskar. Oskar pulled at his chain and started barking.

'You happy now?'

Tat nodded, put his napkin boat on his lap and fiddled with his chicken until my father cut it for him. He was just tying the sailing-boat-napkin round Tat when the phone rang and it was Long-Distance Werner, calling again to spell the name of a town in a country that didn't have an *impending oil crisis*. My father served the second chicken. Henry made little dumplings in his plate, spooned red sauce onto his chicken, spread it like he'd put jam on bread. Silvester winked at me and carefully took from his trouser pocket a paper bird he'd made. It was as yellow as Bird had been, as yellow as the daffodils in Tat's garden in spring and Tat—Tat had finally dozed off.

WITH ONE EAR FIRMLY ON THE PILLOW, I'm lying in bed. The walls are creaking and tapping, the windowpanes rattling, humming, a lorry outside makes the room tremble, a second and third lorry too, then the fridge shakes in the kitchen and it's quiet for a moment.

It's sure to come, sleep, el sueño. It will come through the crack of the door, with Eli's laugh and some light.

THE PEROXIDE BLONDE WAVES from the sofa. The stairwell is brightly lit. Secret whispers. A crystal lampshade is hanging from the ceiling, is making rainbows on the walls, there's the smell of flowers. The Peroxide Blonde is dolling herself up, does her hair in the TV before she turns it on and right up, before the hall starts to spin, the banister to bend, the hall to dance, before the woman from the ground floor helps herself to a cup of coffee that's steaming hot, a cigarette that's lit already and an open book that words fall out of. The cotton wool is still between her toes, my mother notices right away, the nail varnish isn't dry yet for sure, she shakes her head, sweeps up words—a few escape, like little black animals. I hold out my hand but none of them come to me. Eli sits down on the sofa, beside us. Water's running out of the legs of his trousers, his hair is soaking, he's dripping wet, makes everything wet. My mother says he can't stay here like that and he nods and goes. He takes the sound of the television with him. The Peroxide Blonde shakes her head and calls after him.

'The news will be on soon.'

My mother shrugs.

'So what?'

She's eating schnitzel. She licks her fingers and points to where Eli had been standing.

'He's ducking beneath the surface these days.'

'You sure?'

'Guaranteed.'

Blink, even in a dream, blink once and if you're lucky, the image will remain in your head for ever.

GOD IS INTERNATIONALLY FAMOUS. Even the Turk round the corner had a picture of him up. You could see his eye. It was hanging next to a picture of one of the Turk's prophets, of the founder of the Turkish state, and the Swiss flag. My mother sighed every time she'd to wait under the eye of God for her piece of lamb.

The morning after New Year's Day, she stared at the eye for an especially long time and swore the opposite afterwards—the eye had stared at her, had effectively gawped at her, shamelessly, she said, it had asked her, challenged her, to have a final try with God, so he could right any wrong he'd done to her, all those years without ever turning to her. She was furious as she grabbed me by the sleeve and pulled me along behind her to the church where she interrupted the priest who was in the process of taking the crib down. He was scratching fly droppings off Mary and Joseph while Baby Jesus swam in the basin with the donkey and a wise man. Eli wouldn't have liked that. He'd gone to church whenever he could, his faith, in German, had been almost as strong as in Spanish. If I'd told him that, as a child, Jesus had gone for a splash with the donkey and the black wise man, he'd have slapped me one for sure.

My mother took the donkey from the bowl and said that men, even in their old age, don't discover God as he's not much help round the house, that one, and when the priest didn't reply, she complained about not being able to cope with Tat any more and having Tatta round her neck now as well, from the other side—she'd to put a meal out for Tatta, had to iron for her, say hello to her, ask her to join us at the table. She complained too that a house in the mountains was going to rack and ruin. She'd to take care of a house in the mountains that wasn't lived in, and, here, of one that was overcrowded, and of a madman who frightened the neighbours at night, who could see ghosts, who fell over his legs, who put his teeth in the fridge, who peed in the sink. Only a matter of time it was before he went to the zoo and fed his new glasses to the hippo or to the three dogs across the landing.

'And I get stuck with it all.'

The priest was very friendly, he put the brush and Mary down and didn't start shouting or go and lie on the sofa like my father. He asked her to let God help her, said God is here, and she asked where then—is he slumped in front of a telly in the sacristy?

At home, she said:

'God isn't very down to earth.'

She was giving him time.

Two weeks later too, though, God still hadn't made a decision about Tat, and as my father was at a loss anyway, my mother decided she no longer wanted to go round to the Turk and certainly not to the church. For days, she shifted stuff round in the cellar. She gave my father hell about all the scrap wood, the bicycle parts, the broken tools, the crates and small boxes, about the spilt oil, the false windows, the wood shavings, the broom that was in tatters, the shovel with a warp, the paintbrushes steeping in water, the dried-up putty, the pots of paint, the tins and jars, life in general, the cellar in particular, and this whole ramshackle place, in any case, and as my father dabbled round in the soup with his spoon, she confronted him with a choice.

'It's either him or me.'

My father put his spoon down and was on the phone for hours. He consulted with his brothers and sisters, phoned different authorities and the woman next door Tat loved to see and his postman and Madame Jelisaweta and asked me to sit still though I could hardly bear it.

'I don't want Tat to have to go.'

'He doesn't have to go but he's become very peculiar, as you can see yourself.'

'He makes paper boats.'

'Precisely.'

'But they're getting nicer and nicer.'

To Tat, I said:

'They want to put you to sleep'.

He was sitting on his favourite chair. By pulling at a thread, he was undoing the sleeve of his cardigan. His vest was peeking out at the elbow. Fascinated, he looked at the ball of wool in his lap.

'Do you hear me? They want to put you to sleep.'

He just sniggered, pointed at his fleet of tiny boats made from shopping lists and chocolate wrappers and whispered something to Tatta. She must've been very close.

'Tat?'

Most of his time, he spent with her, or in his childhood. He didn't want to hear any more riddles and hadn't solved the last one, not even when I promised to roast apples for him and one for Tatta who must've really fancied a baked apple on the other bank of what he called the Jordan.

'Tat?'

I shook his arm a little.

'They're planning to put you to sleep. Would you not rather do the boat journey you've been planning for such a long time already? On the Jordan?'

Tat looked at me and laughed till he'd tears in his eyes.

'It's not funny. I don't want you to leave.'

He pulled me close and I sank into the apple smell.

EVER SINCE I KICKED THE FENCE, there'd been no calming Oskar any time I went down to clean the hutch. Squeezing his snout between the slats, he'd yelp and yelp, only calming down if I threw him food.

'I haven't got anything, Oskar.'

In my pockets was not even a biscuit crumb. I pulled them out to show him.

'See? Nothing. And now be quiet.'

I opened the hutch carefully and crammed fresh hay in.

'It isn't true Tat's forgetting everything,' I told Snow White. 'It isn't true he doesn't understand anything now. You should've seen him when my father told him just now that his old plum tree had to be chopped down. He took a leg off and battered my father with it. And when my father ran away, Tat threw the leg after him. A perfect throw, it was! You should've heard the crack it made. The Peroxide Blonde opened her balcony door to ask was everything OK. The plum-tree thing has really affected him. Imagine, there was no hay, no hay ever again. Tomorrow, my father's driving him back to the mountains. Tomorrow already. I've to keep him up to date about Milena, Tat says. As exactly as I do you, he says . . . Shut it, Oskar. Just shut it, would you.'

WE TOOK TAT TO THE BARBER'S. His hair was as long as a young rowdy's—and he'd never let anyone near it but Tatta who was dead and therefore somewhat indisposed, as Madame Jelisaweta put it.

My parents went for a coffee and Tat started testing her.

'They want rid of me.'

'Can't imagine that.'

'I keep peeing myself.'

'Can't imagine that.'

'I'm mad.'

'Can't imagine that either.'

'They can though. I forget everything.'

'That may be.'

'I'll forget you too. Once I'm out of here, I'll forget you.'

'Possibly. Be a shame, all the same.'

'Yes, a shame. A big shame. I had a plum tree.'

'With small, firm plums?'

'Indeed.'

'I'd one too. Two, actually.'

'What happened to them?'

'The war ripped one out. My father's.'

'And the other?'

'Tito has it on his conscience.'

'How come?'

'You can't live from plums alone. I'd to leave.'

'I could live from plums alone.'

'At your age, yes. But I was young and needed more to live off. I'd a future in mind, children, something better. Security.'

'So?'

Madame Jelisaweta shrugged.

'Look round you.'

'I couldn't at my age now either.'

'What?'

'Live from plums.'

'Make your mind up, will you?'

'They chopped the tree down. I'd have liked to live for another autumn from the plums.'

'And the rest of the year?'

'From the woman next door. She's still beautiful, even now, Tatta's really jealous.'

I stopped pretending I was sweeping up hair.

'Tatta lives on the other bank of the Jordan. Can't be far from where he lives. Tat wants to go on a boat journey with her.'

'I see.'

'Whippersnapper's a really deep one.'

'And what happened to your legs?'

'Tatta has them already. She doesn't want me taking any more great leaps. I can be quite wild, you know.'

'He'd an accident with his motorbike and then another one with smoking.'

'I see.'

'What's she not like!'

'What's your name anyhow?'

'Tat. Tat Jon. Could you make a start now? I'd like it short. Very short. I want to feel the sun on my skin.'

The Toyota waited outside and Madame Jelisaweta helped Tat out. She'd given him a shave and all and raved about his fine head of hair, full and white. And at his age—almost as rare as a good heart.

Tat behaved properly for the whole journey, almost. First, he stroked the nodding dog on the back shelf, it reminded him of Sepp, and put down, carefully, the small jar of olives Madame Jelisaweta had given him. He talked about her non-stop.

'She did my hair, the stuff on my face too.'

He stroked his clipped moustache and smooth cheeks.

'Like a girl, feel them, like a girl.'

He was quiet while I stroked his cheek. If I stopped, he repeated:

'Feel them, go on—feel them, like a girl.'

I let my hand rest on his cheek and fell asleep. He fell asleep too, woke up, got restless and started talking about this woman who was a real stunner, a natural phenomenon, like the woman next door nearly, never mind Tatta. He reached up and felt his head, nice, he said, she did it nicely, nice. The sun can come out. He shouted:

'I need to go!'

My mother had wrapped herself up to her ears in her rabbit-fur coat and was chewing her nails.

'I need to go. It's urgent. Are you deaf?'

At the next petrol station, my father slammed on the brake so suddenly, it rained olives and the nodding dog went flying against the windscreen. He tore the door open and lifted Tat out. He got him up on his legs and shepherded him to the toilet. I waited outside as Tat yelled at my father inside.

'You could've done something to stop it.'

'What the heck—stop what? You're being impossible again today. Trousers down!'

'They shouldn't have been allowed to chop it down. Not the plum tree.'

'It wasn't bearing fruit any more.'

'Of course, it was bearing fruit. And how. Trees have rest years, you city boy. Killing it off in its sleep! That's what you all did—killed it off in its sleep!'

'What is it you want?'

'I want home.'

'But we're taking you home. Don't go driving everyone mad on me, do you hear? And don't be driving the little one mad either . . . What's wrong now?'

'I can't go if you're standing next to me.'

'I'll head out then. Sit down or you'll fall over.'

'Don't tell me what to do. Not at my age.'

My father stood beside me.

'It's a real pity I gave up smoking more than ten years ago. A cigarette now, what would I give for a cigarette?—What is it?'

'I can't go! Fuckin' prostate.'

'Then give it a miss. Let's go.'

'If you like.'

In the car, Tat peed his trousers. My mother would've put him to bed wet. She wiped the dead flies from the bedspread and was crying so much, she couldn't calm down. Even Tat was embarrassed and said nothing and turned to face the wall.

I asked what *prostate* is and my father, who was tired, replied:

'An organ.'

His answer was a bit lean, I thought, but then I'd seen what happens when there's a *prostate*. I wrote down on a slip of paper:

PROSTATE: causes men grief, makes women sad.

'IT'S BEEN SO QUIET SINCE HE LEFT,' I said to Snow White. 'Tat really kept us on the go, the Peroxide Blonde says. She says he's a bit like the wild animals she only knows from TV otherwise. We're the talk of the town, she says. Other people don't throw their legs round when they're furious. It's something special. Tat is something special.'

I wanted to kick the fence but gave it a miss as Oskar was sleeping.

'Tat can talk. As if it wasn't difficult enough, keeping myself up to date about Milena! Keeping him up to date is impossible by phone. Someone is always there, is being impatient, takes the receiver from me, wants to say something, just wants to ask something quickly, needs to ask something else. Wants to ask how much snow is lying, whether Tat still has firewood in the house, whether Uncle Curdin is looking after him and bringing him firewood, whether the woman next door can look in today or not until tomorrow. Or wants to ask whether Tat is getting up too, putting his legs on, walking round, if he's cooking things, not just polenta, wants to tell him he mustn't forget to give the old polenta to the cats when he cooks fresh stuff. Milena can't stay in the wardrobe for ever, Tat says, and Tat can't stay in the mountains for ever. My mother says he needs to go into a home as he can no longer cope alone. Tat says he's going nowhere. Henry and Silvester offered to ask round their relatives in Africa for a medicine for Tat as they say several people are living within him and that makes his life complicated. They wanted to visit him in the mountains but my father asked them to give it a miss. Given we don't get on with the one God, he doesn't want to involve God knows how many other gods, he says. Too many cooks spoil the broth.'

WE DIDN'T VISIT TAT SO OFTEN ANY MORE, though my father urged us to as Tat didn't have so much time left, in the mountains, before he'd head to Heaven. My father was convinced of it. If we did visit, Tat said nothing all day, nearly, and no longer threw stuff around. On the contrary, he touched the newly knitted sleeve on his cardigan and nodded to my mother, and even if we took him into the garden, he remained seated and his expression didn't ever change. It was as if nothing had anything to do with him any more. If my father asked did he need anything, he said, 'I've got everything.'

The plum tree was the only thing he missed. I turned his chair away from its stump. It made him sad, tears shone in his moustache. Once, he asked me to take him over to it so he could touch it. Together, we'd make it. Tat was almost as light as Snow White, his legs were loose, and my father had to remind him every week to get them adjusted as he was shrinking and getting smaller and smaller and thinner. He forgot. He forgot to light the Toscanis he had in his mouth. He sucked them till they were damp, he sucked them till they were wet, till they crumbled from his lips. He was so forgetful, my mother and father no longer occurred to him either when they were beside his bed, talking to him, fixing his pillows, bringing food to and fro, bringing blankets or taking them away, opening or closing windows. He would blink at them, warily. Only the woman next door could come when she wanted, he'd call out her name and his whole face would beam. Sometimes he beamed when the postman came too—and called the name of the woman next door, he did it again and again, even if my mother came, and when she left the room, offended, I told him he was mistaken, that that had been my mother and she'd brought him a pot full of yellow flowers and a bouillon that was to help him get better, at least, and he took the plate, slowly ate a few spoonfuls, poured the rest into the flowerpot and asked,'How's Milena?'

'She's pale and she's memorizing the heavens.'

He looked at me, puzzled.

'She says the priest says you've more possibilities that way, simply, that Heaven is bigger and reaches further into everything than you think, that any sea you might think of is a puddle, in comparison—the Mariana Trench, just a scratch on the surface, and the head, and all it can think, a pin, nothing, in comparison.'

'That's a matter of opinion.'

'What's more, she says, she'll be able to find her way round better if ever she has to go herself.'

'That's an argument.'

'She says she can't go to church as she can't go anywhere at this moment in time, she says Toni goes for both of them instead. She can use the time to memorize the heavens. She says she already knows how the heavens are constructed, where things are, that suns are ten a penny there, and that there's fog, that the heavens use gas for heating, masses of it, and that you can't get the place to warm cos it's just too big, so big, even the giants don't step on each other's toes. Cos there are "blue giants", you see, as well as "brown dwarfs", Milena says, her encyclopaedia says, and white ones and red ones that have a very hot heart, that no sane scientist trusts, though, cos hearts like that aren't reliable. She says her encyclopaedia says the light of a sun can still be alive, even if the sun's already dead, cos the sun's so far away from us and its light's still on its way to us.'

Tat started to cry. I shook his arm.

'It's not a sad story. It's not a story at all. I didn't make it up. It's all out of a very big encyclopaedia, and the teacher confirmed the stuff about the heavens for me. Mili calls them COSMOS. That's correct too. It's not wrong, at least, the teacher says. COSMOS can also be a word for EVERYTHING.' The tears were dripping from Tat's moustache onto his cardigan.

'Do you want Tatta's picture?'

He shook his head.

'Should I bring you milk and honey?'

Nodding, he reached for the huge hankie under the pillow and blew his nose. When I got back, he was lying there, sleeping, his teeth and legs beside each other on the bedspread.

SOMETHING BURST ON THE STREET, had fallen from the sky, there was a crash that made the windowpanes rattle and putty crumble to the ground. The street shone through the window, the trees were waving their tops, were swaying. What a wind. A lorry was standing at an angle. The baker tried to get out of his new red car that wouldn't stop tooting. It was about half its original length and steam was coming from it. Two men pulled at the door and the baker got out, fell down, got up and went over to the lorry. The driver was leaning against it. People were leaning out of the windows and the clouds were hanging very low. Toni and my mother were down in the street too. Her lovely new coat was flapping in the wind, the two of them really had to brace themselves against it, had to hold hands and disappeared round the corner.

I turned away from the window and snapped the book shut.

A cat climbed onto the Peroxide Blonde's balcony and peed on her basil. Behind the curtain, nothing stirred. It was as if the building was dead. My mother had forgotten her front-door key. It was on the hook.

I packed popcorn, couldn't decide which words to take, opened all the crates, emptied boxes out, still didn't find anything suitable. Finally, I reached for just one word—COSMOS. If you have EVERYTHING with you, there's no need to worry you've forgotten something.

I unlocked the door, carefully, and went in.

Milena was on the floor next to Toni's bed, playing with two large dolls. She got a fright, jumped into the wardrobe and pulled the door shut. I held the bag of popcorn out to her, through the crack.

'Toni's away. My mother is too. Everyone's away. I saw them going. Don't you like popcorn?'

She took the packet from my hand, tore it open. I could hear her chewing.

'It's toffee popcorn.'

The bag rustled again, the popcorn squeaked against her teeth. She wasn't saying anything and I was floundering. I traced the patterns in the wood with my finger.

'Can I see you?'

The door opened a little. She blinked at me.

'You can't stay in there for ever.'

'That's what my father says too.'

She was speaking with her mouth full.

'He often thinks about it.'

'And what?'

'He doesn't know yet.'

'You're speaking better German.'

'I'm memorizing it, like the heavens.'

'Stars that are actually suns.'

'Exactly.'

'COSMOS.'

'Correct.'

'It's not been fully researched yet, the teacher says. You can't memorize it all.'

Mili gave me the once-over. She crumpled the empty packet up and pushed the door open.

'Did you speak to anyone?'

'No, not at all.'

I took the empty packet and put it in my pocket. I couldn't possibly tell her that Tat and Snow White knew. I picked up popcorn crumbs.

'You spoke to the teacher.'

'I didn't. The heavens are the topic at school at the moment.'

That wasn't a lie. The teacher had unrolled a huge blue map with the constellations. Before Christmas, we could've seen a lynx in the sky, at New Year, a big dog, then a unicorn, and soon after that, a mariner's compass—that last one, however, with great difficulty. We could always see the dragon and the Great Bear, the teacher had said, if we wanted.

'You've no idea though.'

'I do. What's more,' I said, 'electric suns have existed for ages.'

'You're lying.'

'I'm not.'

'You are.'

'But we've got one. In bright orange.'

Mili snarled, that's rubbish, and I replied, it was the truth that my mother burns herself at least once a week in the electro sun, her face is then lobster pink for five days and a good colour for two days, and that's without any sky whatsoever. Mili roared:

'I don't believe it!'

'So what,' I roared back. 'I'll go and get it, shall I. I'll show you, you even need to put sunglasses on and can get sunburn like in the mountains, original Swiss sun—just like at strict Uncle Curdin's place in April, my father says. Even he uses it when he's homesick.'

We were glad of everyone who didn't know I was from the Home and my parents childless, that I was a bastard and my parents naive, that I'd no family tree but a stack of records, that they were desperate and I was a hopeless case, that our relationship, in any case, was quite something and, first and foremost, a pure tragedy. Aunt Joujou had seen to it that everyone, up into the Churfirsten, and as far as France, was in the know and the entire town at least had some idea. Mili didn't stop gawping at me.

'What is it now? I want to see it.'

'Coming up.'

I banged the door behind me and ran into the cellar. She was in for a shock. I took all the cables I could find, tucked the sun lamp under my arm, took two steps at once, shot into the flat, then into the bedroom, closed the curtains and set up the sun lamp bang in front of her. I connected the cables and tilted the lid back. Mili shrugged and grumbled, 'It's not exactly big.'

'True,' I said, 'but it makes everything violet.'

I flicked the switch. She took Toni's sunglasses from the bedside table and put them on, we sat down in front of it, the room was violet, I blinked, said, close your eyes, I pulled red glasses with the rubber band over my head, and when we shut our eyes, it was last April and we were sitting outside, at strict Uncle Curdin's place, just the two of us this time, while he and my father were talking in the kitchen and, even just thinking about it, I burnt with shame.

UNCLE CURDIN TAKES MY FATHER TO TASK.

'Why did you bring a woman home who can't have children?'

'We have a child.'

'Come off it, it's an alien you have.'

'Oh yes? What about the people you hid like sacks of potatoes during the war?'

The smoke from Uncle Curdin's cigarette creeps out to us and tickles the inside of my nose. I hear him pacing up and down and Uncle Curdin says, 'That's a long time ago.'

'I remember though.'

'You know about it?'

'Of course I know about it. How daft did you think we were? They lived here, after all.'

'Yes, but I didn't give them my name.'

NO IDEA HOW LONG WE'D BEEN SITTING in the sun at Uncle Curdin's when Mili and I heard the doors opening and my mother said that that was it—she was sick and tired of having to hang around outside in every weather, that she now wanted to sort things out. Then the door opened, she stumbled into the room with Toni, fell over the cables and gasped, 'What's this?'

Toni groaned and I couldn't get a word out. It was quiet for a while until my mother pointed at the sun lamp.

'Is that mine?'

Mili took the huge sunglasses off.

'Who's that?'

Not answering her, like the others were doing, wasn't a good idea. I summoned all my courage up.

'She's a foreign infiltration. Toni has to keep her secret. But she's nice.'

'She's my daughter.'

'You're keeping your daughter secret from me?'

'And she likes popcorn and her favourite colour is green.'

My mother gave me a clout and Toni stepped in front of the wardrobe. She opened the curtains, gave me another clout though I hadn't said anything, gave Toni one while she was at it and looked at Mili who was blinking at the sun. She shook her head, looked at Toni, she'd lost all her colour and said, 'Beyond words! Simply beyond words, this is. Now, *not* is no longer an option. Now, we *have* to speak. Can you see that?'

THE SUN LAMP HAD BEEN SENT FLYING, down into the street. My father was making a thorough job of it—he threw even Toni's holiday photos out of the window. They fluttered down outside Oskar's kennel. Two whole hours, he barked at them. I sat down in the stairwell till it was all over. The Peroxide Blonde passed and said, 'Oh là là!'

Things were in bits on the floor of the kitchen. I gathered them up. Bit by bit, I put together again a plate, a bowl, two cups and, using the other broken pieces, something colourful and completely useless. The glass I threw away.

My father was banging the doors. I went to look for my mother and found her in my room, bent, crying, over my word boxes. All scattered. All empty now. Piles of words, mountains of paper slips, snips, strips, pages, and every one she lifted, she dropped again. What a mess! A sea of words rustling and rushing, knee-high, in my room.

MY FATHER WAS WHISPERING, he was hardly moving his lips, he was speaking on the phone to Tat, wanted to drive to his place, wanted to do away with something he called *antiquated traditions*. He needed to know something cos he wasn't speaking to Uncle Curdin any more, wasn't going to go there any more, only after his death would he go back, to spit on his grave, there was a limit to what he'd put up with, even if it meant missing the house in April.

He wasn't speaking to my mother any more either. She'd to go to Aunt Joujou's in the Churfirsten. Nearly all her clothes went into the suitcase, something for every time of year. She slammed the lid down, cried, tossed some liquorice, all her hellish misery pills and a fresh pair of pants into her handbag. Sewing kit. She threw herself on the bed, pressed a packet of chewing gum into my hand. Cried. Threw me out of the room.

I shoved three chewing gums into my mouth. In the kitchen, my father opened a beer. He called a taxi for my mother, I saw it drive off, heard him going up and down in the kitchen. Standing still.

'Go and feed Snow White. We'll be heading off soon.'

Toni came towards us in the hall. He wanted to turn and go back up, my father dropped everything he was carrying. He was nearly as furious as Natural Disaster could get when he punched Toni in the eye. I forgot to chew my gum, it lay tough and warm in my mouth. The Peroxide Blonde's three dogs were raising the alarm behind the door opposite. Whispering, my father swore it was only cos of Milena he wasn't wringing Toni's neck, he assured him Eli wouldn't have any such inhibitions and would pour him into the foundations of a detached house on some new estate or other, if he ever found out. He then threw the key at his feet, saying, 'Water the damn flowers. We're going to Tat's.'

The Peroxide Blonde came to her door, there was the smell of hairspray, the dogs sneezed and danced round us. My father wanted to wallop the Peroxide Blonde and all and give the dogs to the sausage factory—it was written all over him. The Peroxide Blonde could tell as well, she could see Toni's eye swelling up, above all, and made her excuses. She rounded up her dogs and closed the door quietly and my father told me to spit the gum out.

'Sometime soon, please!'

He stuck it over the Peroxide Blonde's peephole.

Him and Toni were sitting next to each other on the stairs. The light went on, it went off, went on again, flickered. Each time Toni groaned, holding his head, my father gave him a dutch rub, calling him a whoremonger one minute and an arsehole the next, and when Toni, at one point, tried to answer, my father started on him all over again. They stumbled down the stairwell, knocking the macramé owls off the walls, scattering the dried-flower arrangements outside each door, they threw shoes, boots, slippers and dusty doormats at each other, rolled down the stairs, and finally my father kicked at Toni's mailbox till it came off the wall.

I crept into the car, it was cold, I pulled a cardigan over my teddy, put his heaviest cap on, the one my mother had knitted for him, waited and fell asleep.

When my father finally came, it was dark, nearly. The sleeve of his jacket was missing.

'You sleeping? Sorry. I'd to phone the school before we left. If anyone asks, you're sick, OK?'

With his hair full of hay, he drove the road to Tat's in record time. Four times, he'd to stop. Once for the police, the second time cos, after the police, he'd no more money, and the other two times cos I was puking. As he waited, he looked into the rustling pines and drummed his fingers on the car roof.

TAT'S BEDROOM WAS FULL OF FLIES. They came to visit from the cowshed next door, buzzed round him, then weren't able to find their way back. When they got tired and fell on his bed, he'd crumble them up, wipe the crumbs from the bedspread, wonder where all the soot was coming from when there was no heating in the room. He asked for milk and honey, and his cardigan.

My father wanted to know about the married couple that had lived at Uncle Curdin's during the war, the *whole* story. He wanted the exact details, the 'before and after', how the Rhine was flowing, what the water level was, what the nights by the Rhine were like, back then when Tat kept the nights secret, sometimes whole days too.

'Will you show us photos?'

'Be quiet, you.'

'Leave her alone—there aren't any photos from back then, what are you thinking? Wasn't it always dark? In all of Switzerland, it was dark,' said Tat. 'I don't want to talk about it, actually.'

'Why not?'

'You don't win any prizes with that nowadays either. Look at them—they want to keep Switzerland clean of anything from outside it. Seeing as you're here, though, could you fix two clocks for me? They're in the kitchen. Go and get them.'

My father sighed.

'But you've some that do work.'

'But those two in the kitchen don't. I need them.'

'How are your legs?'

'Wonderful. They both hurt.'

Tat was tired though he was sleeping well, sometimes in the daytime too. Tatta's been quiet for days, he said. She wasn't whining any more, nagging him about the Jordan any more. She was letting him sleep, letting him sit in peace. In the garden, Tat now occasionally took a leg off again, watched the crocuses grow, and rubbed his stump.

TAT HAD KEPT AN EYE ON THE BORDER at the Rhine. That was his occupation. The Rhine wasn't leak-proof, not its 'old arm', as he called it, not during the war Herr Hitler had provoked, the war my mother and the whole of France were involved in as well. Switzerland was afraid of getting involved too, it kept out of it and would've been happy not to let anything in that wasn't gold, Tat said.

That said, what was wading and swimming over by night, even before the war, wasn't gold, he said. It was wet, it was wheezing, it was freezing, it was shivering, it was calling for its mother or son or wife. You'd to hold a hand over their mouths if one had gone missing. They also came alone sometimes. They didn't say anything, remained silent for days, hardly ate and would've let you do anything to them but one thing—they didn't want to turn back. Most of them were people called *Jews*. Once they'd arrived in Switzerland, Tat called them *refugees*.

When Herr Hitler later started rounding them up, all over Europe, and word got round he was doing it to kill them and take their gold teeth, they tried even more to cross the border where Tat was stationed. He couldn't say no.

'What else was I supposed to do? I turned a blind eye if I picked them up over in Lustenau or pulled them out of the water if they'd lost their way at the bridge, the lido, or if they came through the Pipe. They could spend one night at our place. Tatta gave them dry clothes and polenta. The next night, I'd take them to Uncle Curdin. He'd a house and, unlike me, no children.'

'That's right, even back then, no one—if they'd any choice—visited Uncle Curdin,' my father said. 'He'd a reputation in the village for sudden rages.'

'Curdin kept them till they could continue to St Gallen or Zurich. Generally, they wanted to continue immediately. Don't ask me how they managed to. I've no idea . . . Careful with the glass—it's old.'

'Let me get on with it just.'

Tat leant back. The glass in the frame rattled when my father closed it, to turn the clock round.

'When are you going to make coffee?'

'When I'm done with the clocks. Keep going.'

To begin with, it wasn't difficult to become a refugee, Tat continued. But very soon, Switzerland banned it as it was unhappy with Austria fleecing the Jews, and them then—whatever the weather—stumbling into Switzerland in a hurry, with their small suitcases and empty pockets.

'I'd really like a coffee now.'

My father threw the screwdriver and tweezers onto the little table and went into the kitchen. Tat called after him, 'With lots of milk! See and heat it first. And three lumps of sugar!'

'Keep going.'

'And don't go thinking, by the way, that trips into Switzerland were free. Quite a few here earned a fair amount that way. The Nazis had taken almost everything from them, the people smugglers took the rest. I don't know what Curdin earned. It certainly wasn't little.'

'What are *Nazis*? And *people smugglers*?'

My father came in with the coffee grinder just as Tat was drawing breath before explaining the *Nazis* to me.

'And you? Did you make money out of them too?'

'Come on, tell me, what are *Nazis*? And *people smugglers*?'

Tat didn't answer. He too knew the condition he liked to say my mother had—the overwrought-nerves-phase. You could see it by the two different colours in his face. His face was red, his nose white, and he was chewing his moustache.

'I'm only going to tell you this once.'

'And only the way it suits you to.'

'Do you remember the Sonne?'

'The restaurant?'

'If they still had any, the last of their money was counted there. To begin with, they came with their families, then as couples, the children would follow later, three months later, maybe four. Those who had made it here wakened us at night because their relatives had been loitering round the other bank for days. Parents followed, an uncle, aunts. Then no one wakened us any more, we'd wake ourselves. They arrived more and more dispersed, more and more hungry, with eyes like lunar lakes, I tell you, never did they have papers and only rarely did they still have photos with them, or maps of where it was easiest to cross—right beside the bridge, the water only up to your ankles, the stones as slippery as oiled wood,' said Tat. 'Or at the lido. We fetched them on the other side. It was getting more and more dangerous, the Germans knew too, sure, and Tatta was giving me hell—there were thirteen of us to be fed after all. But what were we supposed to do? Send them back? Where? And then talk big in the Sonne like the roofer or the shoemaker who would gladly have bootlicked the Nazis and were already seeing themselves as Gauleiters?'

Were *Nazis*, *people smugglers* and *Gauleiters*, maybe also *refugees*, wanting to follow on? I didn't dare to ask. Tat cursed and was spitting as he spoke. His dentures didn't fit properly.

'Huora cac! What absolute swine! Tatta didn't want to let them go until she'd darned their trousers. But then they'd to go to Uncle Curdin. If he'd no space, they walked over the fields, to meet someone or other somewhere or other. I watched them go. They still niggle at me nowadays, turn up in my dreams, disappear and return the following night. I didn't ever want to know their names. Now, I'd like to. To begin with, some helped with the peas, though that was also forbidden.'

'When was "to begin with"?'

'Summer of '38.'

'I barely remember.'

'You were a child. Flying a kite was more important. What about the coffee?'

'It's almost ready.'

'My mouth's dry.'

'I said, I'm almost ready.'

Tat banged the floor with his stick till my father returned with the coffee.

'There are still biscuits. Beside the cooker.'

'Those are mouldy.'

'You sure?'

'They're grey!'

'Whatever. Sit down and listen.'

'You wanted coffee.'

Tat slurped slowly from the saucer.

'Too much milk. Can I have another sugar?'

'You've got three lumps already.'

'But there's too much milk in it. That means I need more sugar.'

My father looked at me.

'Tat wants more sugar.'

I went to the kitchen on tiptoe, so as not to miss anything. The sugar was on the top shelf. I'd to fetch a chair. When I finally had the tin in my hands, I heard Tat ask:

'Where was I?'

'Summer of '38.'

'Yes. Soon after that, the soldiers came. Getting people across became more and more dangerous. A lot wanted over the border.'

'Switzerland was neutral.'

'Neutral? Don't make me laugh! It had to be profitable, for a start. That's a load of shit!'

'*Please*, the little one—'

'Nonsense! Whippersnapper's old enough to hear it.'

'Oh yeah? And we weren't? You could've told us what you were up to.'

'Are you mad? You know about the list, don't you? The execution orders? The shoemaker who was already seeing himself as a Gauleiter—'

'Yes, yes, you said already.'

'Yes, I did. If it had ever come to that, you see, he'd have shot us dead, personally. Curdin, me and a few others. Imagine, the shoemaker had shot me—I don't even know, is he still alive?'

'You've something hanging there.'

'Where?'

'In your moustache. Crema.'

Tat wiped his whole face.

'Is there any more coffee?'

Again my father looked at me.

'Tat would like more coffee.'

'With four lumps of sugar. You know, it was just the once someone came from Berne to hear what the people from across the border had to report—so it's said, anyhow. I'm sure we'd already washed and fed those he got to see. They'd had a sleep and had already written their first letters. To America. Why are you asking me all this? Why do you suddenly want to know?'

Tat unstrapped a leg and scratched at his stump. I couldn't stop myself from at least asking:

'Did all *refugees* have teeth made of gold?'

'No.'

My father raised his hand, Tat stopped him.

'A married couple stayed on at Uncle Curdin's.'

'I know.'

'He was a doctor from Vienna, she was from Paris, originally. We called them Madame and Monsieur, and they invited us to join them for some pie in the back room, I've no idea how long Madame had put food aside at the time to make it, food she borrowed—*borrowed*—from Tatta. Never before and never since have I eaten pie like it. Have you, maybe?'

'I wasn't there.'

'Weren't you? Oh, I thought—It was Monsieur who gave me the schnitzel recipe. The original. Using veal.

After the war, I made them using his recipe—not Tatta, me. We'd only talked about it, previously. Monsieur spoke about coating them with breadcrumbs, about flour, about eggs and breadcrumbs, about deep-frying them, and a smell he could describe in a way that had it reaching my nostrils as we stood in the cornfield in the marsh, waiting to receive some.'

'In the marsh across the border?'

'Of course. it belonged to us, that spot of land. The war didn't change that either. I taught you how to make schnitzel.'

'I know.'

'Do you still make them?'

'On special occasions.'

My father put the screwdriver down and closed the front of the clock.

'That's that sorted. It's ready to run a race again.'

He wound both clocks up and took them into the kitchen. When, one after the other, all four cuckoos cuckooed, I heard him say, 'Perfect.' Tat was a long way off, seemed to be thinking about something. He then gave me a long look.

'He knows?'

I nodded.

'So? What's he planning to do?'

Tat tilted his head as he always did when something was too quiet and he couldn't hear though he was trying his hardest.

WITH MY EAR FIRMLY ON TWO PILLOWS, I'm lying in bed. Sleep doesn't want to come. My father can't get to sleep either. He turns on the light. All sleep is with Tat. He's talking in his sleep. To Tatta. To Sepp.

We're waiting. My father knows the word for sleep in many languages.

'In Surselvan too?'

'La sien.'

I think of Eli. My father gives me a questioning look.

It's sure to come, sleep.

'El sueño.'

'THE PEROXIDE BLONDE HAS GOLD TEETH TOO.'

'She brought them into the marriage with her.'

'Had she no teeth before?'

'She did, but none made of gold. They're her dowry. Her father had them made.'

'What's *dowry*?'

'Something like an income.'

'Will you have gold teeth made for me too?'

'No.'

'But I also need an income.'

'School will help you with that.'

'I'll get some from school?'

'In a way, yes.'

'Will the Germans pull our teeth too when we're dead?'

'No, they won't be pulling anyone's teeth any time soon again.'

'Are you afraid of them?'

'No. Not any more.'

'Were you never afraid again?'

'On the contrary.'

'Are you ever afraid now?'

'Yes, every day.'

'What of?'

'Not having the strength.'

'To do what?'

'Ask questions as simply as Tat.'

'When?'

'About the things that are most important.'

'IT'S COLD.'

'Then wait in the car.'

My father came out from behind the bush and pulled up the zip in his trousers. He looked out at the lake for a while. I turned my back to him and looked up the mountain.

'I don't want to go there.'

'But we're almost there.'

'Still.'

'Tat will manage on his own. We're going to fetch your mother.'

'Still.'

'And why not?'

'They don't like me.'

'Sooner or later, they will.'

If he hadn't sent my mother away, we wouldn't have to go to fetch her again. To this village. By the lake.

The mountains stood there like back teeth, rising into the sky. The village had nowhere to grow. Either it would hit against the wall or fall into the lake. A lake like a groove in the landscape, my father said, filled with water, and with fish in it that are as old and as shrewd as Tat and Confucius combined. Not even a road took you there. You had to take the boat.

Aunt Joujou was proud of the water, its colour, of the mountains close behind her, of her scaly house stuck to the slope and of the wine that grew there, almost like in France.

Tat didn't like the lake, the mountains—they weren't his. And water that didn't go anywhere he found boring. The wind gave him a headache, he called the wind a SMALADIU GIAVEL, a blasted devil, a word that in the Encyclopaedia of Good Reasons filled entire pages.

Aunt Joujou's house looked out onto the lake, the sun burnt down onto its face all day. So it wouldn't have to screw up its eyes, they'd installed small windows from the start. On the ledges, my aunt grew red flowers, the nicest in the village. I wrote down *geraniums*, and put them in with PHILODENDRON, DAFFODIL/NARCISSUS, COWSLIP, DAISY, MARIGOLD, ASTER, HAWTHORN, BLACKTHORN, CHESTNUT, HORSE CHESTNUT, FIR, FIG, SPRUCE, CEDAR, BLACK-EYED SUSAN, STRAWBERRY, ROSEMARY, SAGE and PLUM TREE.

The word boxes had always been lost on Aunt Joujou. She rummaged round in them and asked, 'Why's she doing that? Her head not enough on its own?'

'And why have you a Bible? Can't believe without it?'

They growled at each other, anyone else would've run out of the house but we were accustomed to this, thanks to Uncle Curdin, who could've learnt a thing or two from Aunt Joujou when it came to making lifelong enemies in a matter of seconds.

She wiped her hands on her apron, snapped 'very well then', snatched the FLOWERS box from me and began sorting them: BLACK-EYED SUSAN, DAFFODIL/NARCISSUS, ASTER, MARIGOLD, GERANIUM.

'At least do it properly. *Garden Flowers* and *Wild Flowers*, *Deciduous Trees* and *Coniferous Trees*. That's how to do it.'

'Why does your house have scales? Does it have to swim?'

'What are you thinking? Those are called *shingles*. Write it!'

Aunt Joujou licked her fingers and counted the slips of paper like my mother would Tat's savings in the tin can. I wrote *shingles* and thought SCALES. Again and again, when there was a storm, the lake would feel like licking the grapes, together with the sticks, off the slope, like climbing the mountain, washing away the grass, a jetty, a house. Aunt Joujou went to town whenever the subject turned to storms, storms were her *métier*, especially *foehn storms* and very especially *Walensee foehn storms*.

'It can get really wild, the Walensee. Foehn is rare here but when it does come, it hits everything. It carries whole trees down to the lake. The tourists get goose pimples when they see the big roots sticking out of the water, they get goose pimples from the wind that hounds the boat across the lake, and they get goose pimples from the story that here, and nowhere else in Switzerland, a steam boat sank, sank without trace, the bank swallowed up by waves as high as mountains. And above the mountain-high waves, the Churfirsten, swallowed up by cloud-mountains, no jetty in sight, no wood, just raging water and a hissing tub, a howling storm—the tourists have felt uneasy on the crossing ever since. Even if there's a breeze, they get uneasy—and they're right to—and they're glad when they step onto dry land here again, or over there, on the other side, where they jam the road on Sundays. Yes, the wind can just be playing here, and suddenly it gets frisky and the lake starts to smell different, to smell of seaweed, of fish, as if it was opening all the windows before starting to cook.'

Aunt Joujou was finished counting the words I'd brought with me. Tidy little piles, ordered according to size, with an elastic band round each.

'*Voilà*! And now I'll put the char in foil. Fresh from the lake. Your parents will go for a drive and no doubt have a thing or two to discuss. You can help me with the fish.'

THE LAKE ISN'T WARM, isn't friendly, it's never that in summer either. It's too restless for that, my father said. Aunt Joujou's relatives were restless too and unfriendly. They could look at you such you'd get cold feet and sweaty hands. Tat said the lake's constant coldness and shitty mood carried over onto the people.

'And if I stop to think about it,' Tat had said with a grin, 'that has soul. Write me a postcard from there, will you?'

My mother was lake-restless, and my father too. They'd sailed through the groove in the landscape, brushing the water against the fur, in the small boat, on the uncle's large barge, the cousin's bark or the aunt's boat. They'd caught the water bug, there's no avoiding the water here, Tat's right, they all get like the lake, that's how they sat at the table. Waves and light licked the ceiling, cool and green, and while the scaly house chirruped in the warmth, they'd no doubt discussed a thing or two, just as they were now saying nothing.

Aunt Joujou opened the windows. My mother rubbed her temples.

'The foehn won't hold up. It will collapse. You've got to stay.'

Dear Tat,

Why I don't like writing postcards is: my letters don't have space, to say nothing of words. In the Encyclopaedia of Good Reasons, there has been a further reason against postcards since today. The wind has swept the kiosk into the lake, the uncles are fishing for postcards, and the fish are reading yesterday's paper, are chewing gum. Everything's full of water—the lake overflowed last night, and we're staying a day longer though the boat could get up closer to the house today, and the gum-chewing fish are maybe hiding from the fishermen under the Toyota in the car park across the lake. They're as shrewd here as you and Confucius combined.

My father has to think. My mother says just not to think too long, or I'll go down the drain on them, at the last minute. Ruth and Walter invest children only in whole marriages, not in broken ones. The Housemother had said that as well. Eli and all. I don't want to go down the drain. If need be, I'll go to Uncle Curdin. None of Eli's friends can take me into their homes, they're moonlighting enough as it is.

Aunt Joujou has just one clock and sometimes even forgets to wind that one up. She must have a special time-secret she keeps in the Churfirsten somewhere. They're full of water too. In the spring, they sweat it out. I've seen photos with jagged edges, as jagged as the Churfirsten. In them, the uncles are hanging on ropes in the rock when they're not fishing or sailing gravel round the lake.

The lake is a SMALADIU GIAVEL.

I've been thinking too.

Who all has a soul:

The Housemother.

The Housemother's dog.

Helene and everything she cooked.

My mother.

My father.

Toni, even if my father can't believe it.

Milena.

Eli.

His name: Eliseo Álvaro Manuel Raúl Caballero Pardo.

His curses.

Blackberries from the river bank.

The Peroxide Blonde.
You.
Paper boats.
Tatta, who is nothing but soul now,
like Sepp,
like Bird,
and the woman downstairs.
Henry and Silvester.
Dejan and his guitar.
Mirela and her silhouette.
Madame Jelisaweta
and all the hair she collects.
How she collects it.
Her Uncle Jernej who is now a fish,
a lot of fish.
The fish in the river.
The fish in all the rivers,
in all the seas.
The fish in all the lakes.
All the lakes
apart from the Walensee
and those who fish in it.

Make a paper boat just for me.
Whippersnapper.

AUNT JOUJOU AND MY MOTHER WERE STANDING, smoking, at the jetty. We were paddling our rubber boots in the water till the boat came.

Aunt Joujou waved, the uncles waved. We were on the large barge. They hadn't slipped us any fish. My uncles hadn't caught any.

My father knelt and looked under the car, kicked the tyres and felt the paintwork, but apart from a mud crust as far up as the wheel hub, clumps of grass on the bonnet, and loads of birdshit on the roof, he couldn't find any storm damage. He plucked grass from the bonnet and walked round the Toyota. As my mother used a hankie to touch the door handle, he couldn't stop shaking his head.

'Beyond words! Look at that.'

He banged the door shut, started the Toyota and listened for a few minutes to the growling, buzzing and chugging of the engine before he drove off. With cheeks as red as the peaches in Tat's garden, my mother watched my father drive, as if he were doing magic. She flicked her cigarette out of the window. She'd been watching like that all morning already. She and my father seemed to be enjoying themselves, greatly. He whistled and hummed until my mother put in a cassette. The lake threw its blue at the wet rock faces and they dripped, the water running from the rock onto the road.

A bend in the road swallowed the lake. The blue was away. Gone. Sun was shining in our faces, and my father said, 'I don't get why they poach the char in foil. Chervil butter is what you should serve it with. A soupçon of chervil butter. Frothed.'

No letter from Tat and no phone call. One, just, from the woman next door. Tat had put his phone on the stove, trying to make coffee, she said. Otherwise, everything was fine. He liked to sleep in the sun. The cats took turns on his lap. She'd to look for him in the garden every evening. Being angry didn't help. He'd just smile at her, she told us. Would, first, ask for his teeth and a little patience. My father was satisfied.

'He's looking after himself.'

My father held the receiver out to me. The woman next door said:

'He carries your letter round with him. Day and night. Wait, I'll put him on.'

'Whippersnapper, is that you?'

He cursed his head that would even let him drink a melted phone and was about to write a shopping list for the next day. He wrote like a snail. Always started his shopping lists the day before so they'd be ready when the woman next door came.

With one ear firmly on the pillow, I'm lying in bed. The walls are creaking and tapping, the windowpanes rattling, humming, a lorry outside makes the room tremble while the words in my head curl up, get warm and fall through the floor, the floors, into the snow behind Tat's house, where Bird is sitting, singing. I blink. Tat's making coffee with the house, it starts to smell of baked apples while he's in the garden, sleeping, the cellar's in flames already, and the woman next door has to drop the shopping, it's as if she's struck by lightning, nearly. In her arms, she holds a burnt-black, happy Tat, who absolutely *has* to give her an apple, freshly baked and sweet—he wants to give the whole world apples and the woman next door another kiss. It's one of many. They give off light and fire, bright stars, sparks. Turn night into day.

It came quite unnoticed, sleep, el sueño.

WE'RE DRIVING AT NIGHT, are wearing our pyjamas and cardigans in the car. My father is silent. He gets out of the Toyota, checked. My mother, striped. The woman next door is standing there, flowery. She's got out of her bed too. Tat, alone, is lying on the couch, as if he's about to get married again. All the clocks have stopped. On the windowsill are six letters, each labelled in ink. My father reads out: 'Neighbour, Son, Whippersnapper, Daughter-in-law, The Others, Insurance.'

The woman next door, pale, stands in front of my father. She's tired, her black eyes check round the kitchen. She gratefully accepts my father's hankie. He's crying, my mother's crying. Without looking, they dig in their pockets for more hankies. No one thought of taking any with them. My mother hands him a fresh pair of pants from her handbag. He tears them in pieces.

'For when you're on the move. You never know, do you.'

The woman next door nods sympathetically and sobs. Everyone's sobbing, they sigh, they go and make coffee and stir it till it's cold. Crying, my father throws something else out of the window that should've been thrown out long ago. He touches the letters on the windowsill and sits down at the table again. The door opens, wind blows in, milk vapours and the smell of cheese, the smell of wet sheep. Uncle Curdin arrives, no one knows where from. How he knows Tat has died, no one can say either. Some people from the village arrive, knock the muck from their shoes and sit down, join the others. The ringing of cups and spoons. No one wants to wind up a clock. It's not the done thing, the woman next door says.

'Put more wood on.'

The stove is glowing, the wood is crackling, they lower sugared strings into their coffees, amber-coloured chains they suck at. Clear, sprinkled with spots, as warm as Tat's eyes that he now keeps shut. With both cheeks full of rock candy, I close my eyes. For a brief moment, everything's sweet.

They light candles. Again and again, someone sits down beside Tat on the couch and speaks to him. I have to get up and make space. My mother is restless. Her hands are in her lap, holding each other tight, her knuckles are nearly as white as Tat's.

'What a wind! It will sweep Tat away before it's time.'

My father takes his spoon out of the cup.

'When is the right time?'

'When he's at peace.'

It's the first thing Uncle Curdin has said. Only then does he take his hat off and look to and fro, now into the fire, now at Tat. The woman next door takes my hand in hers.

'He's still here.'

'Tat's still here?'

'Of course. But he'll be leaving us.'

'When?'

'Soon. You need to say goodbye to him.'

She goes out into the wind and comes back in, her hair pointing in all directions. She brings in the ones who call Tat Nonno. They kiss colourful pictures and put them down on his suit, push them into his pockets. Jesus in all different colours, on the cross and in Heaven, Mary and the fat child that was once Jesus are on Tat's collar.

My father doesn't like this.

'Tat isn't even a Catholic. And anyway, he thinks all that is tripe.'

The woman next door looks at him.

'But the others don't. Now is about the others.'

It's almost morning already and the ones who call him Grandfather won't arrive until noon cos they don't drive like my father. You can only reach the Churfirsten quickly by water, France first has to meet up, and Eli won't be coming. The sun rises as the Peroxide Blonde phones three times, asking each time for my mother. She's standing in front of our wardrobe at home, will be bringing clothes with her, and Madame Jelisaweta. Tat needs another haircut and the best Slibowitz.

I need Tat.

I need the Encyclopaedia of Good Reasons from front to back.

I need Tat to call after me, to shout 'Whippersnapper!', to hold out his hand and wink, to keep his amber eyes open and curse, curse like mad, curse like a trooper, curse till the cats start to cower, till the wind stops, promises, indeed, to mend all the tiles it has broken, not even an hour did it need for all that damage. I want the clocks to start ticking with shock, the chains to rattle, the fir cones to hop, the clocks to make up the hours they slept through. I want the hands to run, and the works to sweat lubricating oil so that their cuckoos purr through all the rooms, the cuckoos spit one single 'Cuckoo!' from their beaks, and Tat back to life—away from where he is now, away.

I want to hear all his curses.

The one for the postman: Buglia ladg!

The ones for the insurance: Lumpamenta! Bargada! Bastardaglia!

For the people whose names he has forgotten but not what they did: Pitoc! Bastard! Carugna! Canaglia! Tgau Pentel!

Those for every thing and every occasion: Huora cac! Miarda! Grascha putana! Miarda di giat! Zacher Giavel!

I'd like to smell him.

The smell of apple, the smell of wool, leather and hair. But Tat is cold, the apple smell has flown away, I take off my glasses to look for him but he isn't there any more. AppleWoolTat has gone, has taken everything with him, and I can't see even what I need. Falling, I pull one of his legs off.

It is Slibowitz that wakes me and Madame Jelisaweta's perfume sends me off to sleep again.

It is my mother who wakes me and an apronful of apples she puts down beside my head sends me off to sleep again.

It is my father who wakes me and says, 'It's time.'

The woman next door is serving coffee.

'We can't do any more for him.'

My father blinks at the light.

'And for Milena?'

I whisper it in his ear.

My father nods.

It is daylight, the house a hive that's humming. They're speaking Surselvan, Italian, French and German, I don't let Tat out of my sight, I want to see him leaving us.

EPILOGUE

Sometimes, I put Tat's glasses on and read his letter. The paper boat swims before my eyes. The handwriting, even more so.

Whippersnapper!

I have to go. Avoid the Jordan for a while. Other than that, go for it.

Eternally,

Your Tat Jon.